SOMETHING LIKE LUST

PIPER RAYNE

Cover Design: Luniander

Illustration: Valendtin Lebedenko

1st Line Editor: Joy Editing

2nd Line Editor: My Brother's Editor

Proofreader: My Brother's Editor

ABOUT SOMETHING LIKE LUST

Do it.

Don't do it.

Never in my life did I think I'd wager in my head whether to sleep with Chicago Grizzlies wide receiver, Damon Siska.

He's the perfect package—hot body, killer smile, and flirts like he earned a doctorate in it. But anyone who reads gossip blogs knows he is looking for one amazing night and nothing more.

I'm not the usual type of woman he beds. I'm a middle school teacher who cherishes her quiet nights in, drinking wine, and watching romantic comedies, dreaming I'm the heroine. I'm not embarrassed to admit— I want the fairy tale.

But Damon caught me at a weak moment. Fresh off a break-up and feeling lousy about myself, I gave into temptation and left the next morning like every other woman he'd slept with.

Except I walked away with more than just the memories when three weeks later the little white stick glowed with two pink lines.

SOMETHING LIKE *Lust*

CHAPTER 1
DAMON

No wonder I had to hire a private investigator to find her. The woman who randomly texted me to tell me she's having my baby lives in bumfuck nowhere.

I press on the gas after the hundredth four-way stop intersection, pull into the parking lot of Morning Roots Middle School, and park along the curb by the front door. I climb out of my Mercedes G Class and walk toward the doors, pocketing my keys. Damn, I think it's even colder out here than in the city. I pull my jacket tighter around me until I reach the large entrance to the school.

I tug on the first door.

Locked.

I go to the other door.

Locked.

What the hell?

I glance over my shoulder at the parking lot full of cars. It's Wednesday. I move to the final door and reach for the handle.

"Can I help you, sir?" a woman's voice asks.

I scan the area around me. No one is here.

"The speaker, sir." The woman's voice is curt. "To your right."

I look over, and sure enough, there's a silver box with a sign that says, "Press here to enter."

"I'm here to see someone," I say into the microphone.

"And who would the someone be?" Her clear annoyance only irritates me.

Sorry I don't know the rules of the speaker. When I was young, you just walked into the school. Of course, it was a private academy. I never attended a public school. And times have changed.

"Adeline Morgan." There's a long pause,

so after a minute or so, I press the button. "Hello?"

"I'll be with you in a minute," she snipes.

My head rears back from the speaker. "Well then," I mutter to myself.

"I can hear you," she says.

"Not making any new friends today, Siska," I grumble, stuffing my hands in the pockets of my jacket. Does this lady remember it's February in Illinois? Probably the coldest month of the year?

I should be on vacation right now. The one I always take when football season is over. I should be celebrating winning the championship game with my team. I should be on a sandy beach with the sun beating down, a woman on each side of me.

Where I should not be is in the middle of nowhere with two inches of snow on the ground and whipping wind that chills every bone in my body, which is still healing from a rough season. I should not be so nervous about this impending conversation that it feels as if my breakfast is going to make a reappearance.

The buzzer goes off, though the woman's voice doesn't come through the speaker at all, so I rush to pull open the door. I enter a small foyer and am presented with another set of doors. Once I'm through there, I'm standing in front of the woman behind the voice—based on the sour expression on her face. A man behind her wears a big security badge, but his smile says he's a Grizzlies fan.

"You're lucky I have fast reflexes," I say.

"Actually, you're lucky you do." She doesn't offer even a tight smile.

Not wanting to deal with any more bull-shit from this lady, I get right to the point. "Is Adeline Morgan around?"

"She's teaching. Did you miss the sign outside?"

If this lady's attitude was directed at anyone else, I'd find this funny, but I've had maybe an hour's sleep over the last two nights. I won the championship and couldn't even celebrate with my team be-cause my mind kept coming back to that text I received right after our win.

I'm pregnant, and you're the dad.

The clearing of a throat pulls me back to the present and the snarky lady in front of me.

"Can you call her and ask to come here?"

She blows out a breath. "We do not make it a habit to interrupt our teachers for non-emergencies. Is this an emergency?"

I'd like to say yes, but in the conventional sense, the answer is no.

She raises her hand, snapping her fingers. "Elijah, come here."

A boy I hadn't seen standing behind her, and the security guard walks out from around them. He has a young, innocent face that's starting to grow a mustache. He stares at me, and I smile at him.

"What's up?" I ask.

He doesn't respond, his unblinking eyes steady on me.

I return my gaze to the woman. "Listen, tell her Damon Siska is here. I think she'll want to see me."

That's likely a lie, given the fact Adeline hid her pregnancy from me for six months. I doubt she wanted me to show up where she works, but I prefer the element of surprise. Giving anyone knowledge of what you're about to do gives them time to prepare, think of an out.

"And what makes you so special?" the woman asks.

Feeling the kid's eyes on me still, I glance down and offer him a fist bump. He slowly raises his small fist and knocks mine before lowering it, all while not blinking.

I want to tell her to ask this kid why I'm so damn special or the guy behind her—who must be scared of her too—because I see his excitement in the smile he's still giving me.

She frowns and waves for me to follow her into the office on her right. I do so, as do the security guard and the kid. We all stand on the opposite side of a desk as her while she lowers her head and writes a note, strips it off a pad, and holds it out over the desk.

"Elijah, take this to Miss Morgan, please." She turns her gaze to me. "You can have a seat." She points with her pen behind me.

"Why don't I just go with Elijah?"

She scoffs. "This is a school, sir."

"You can call me Damon," I offer with the hope she'll give me her name. Maybe if we're on a first-name basis, we could make this run a little smoother.

"No, thank you. As I was saying, this is a

school. We don't let just anyone who wanders in walk around the school."

I open my mouth, but she's quick to put up her hand. This woman reminds me of Mrs. Labyrinth in twelfth grade when she caught me in her basement with her daughter. She made my life miserable in physics class that year.

"Now, I know you're Damon Siska. I recognized you as you stepped out of your fancy car after you decided you were too important to park in the lot like the rest of us and felt like the fire lane was what you deserved. Obviously, Elijah thinks you're all that and a bag of chips. Usually the kid can't shut up. But no one is going to walk through our school unless they clear through me."

Begrudgingly, I sit in one of the plastic chairs, officially schooled. Everyone always likes me, so why does this woman have a problem with me? Then it dawns on me…

"You're a Green Bay fan!" I point in her direction, and the security guy nods. "That makes sense. We're kind of close to the border of Wisconsin, right? That's cool. I have some friends who play up there, even if we're rivals. Who's your favorite player? I can get you an autograph or maybe tickets." The season's over, so I can't really offer her much at the moment. But Roman Maxwell plays for them now after being traded from the Grizzlies a couple years ago.

"This has nothing to do with what football team I cheer for. There are rules, and based on your reputation, I gather you don't like to follow them."

I point at myself and look over my shoulder. "I'll have you know, in kindergarten, I received the best listener award."

She stares blankly while the security guard laughs but is quick to stop when she gives him a scathing look over her shoulder. "Are you looking for a congratulations?"

"Nope. Just stating facts." I sit back in the uncomfortable seat and wait.

The longer I wait, the more my bravado ebbs, and my nerves set in. I crack my neck a few times. Seriously, the drive here sucked. Why would anyone want to live here? There's nothing here for a single woman Adeline's age. Especially one so beautiful.

I sit in silence for at least ten minutes, observing the woman's demeanor with other people who come in. She's pleasant to a mom bringing in her son's lunch because he left it at home. She smiles at a father here to pick up his sick kid. And she's downright flirtatious with the package delivery guy, purposely eyeing me as she apologizes to him about the parked car in the fire lane.

He smirks at me when he turns to leave but stops in his tracks. "Damon Siska?"

I nod. "Hey, man."

"Damn." He pats himself down, looking for a pen. I know that's what he's doing because it's a common occurrence. "Shit, my pen is in the truck." He turns back around, and dragon lady already has a pen and paper out for him. "Thanks, Shaylene." He takes it from her and turns back to me. "Do you mind?"

"Not at all. I'm nice like that." I eye Shaylene, then sign Go Grizzlies and my name.

"Thanks. My son is at the high school and he's gonna die when I tell him that you were here. Why are you here?" He scours the area as if there should be a chalkboard with the reason displayed for him to read.

"Just visiting a friend."

He nods. "Awesome." He holds up the paper. "Thanks for this."

Elijah walks back into the office, his face red. He averts eye contact with me, handing a note to Shaylene. "She wrote you a note back, Ms. Gregory." His head falls down so his chin rests on his chest.

She reads it. I want to rush across the room and grab it from her to read it myself.

"As I thought." She tears up the paper. "She's busy with her classes today. She said she'll call you later."

My mouth drops open. "Seriously?" I approach the desk, wanting to grab the small pieces of paper and assemble them to see what she really said. I've never been good with being kept out of the inside circle.

"I'm not sure what you expected. This is a school. Miss Morgan is a teacher and therefore is here to teach the children who attend. She cannot just walk out of her classroom to see what you need."

Elijah's shoulders slowly rise as if he wishes he could sink into the floor. The feeling is mutual.

I hold up my hands. "Fine. I get it. Let me at least leave my number." I eye the pen and paper the delivery guy left, and she sighs before handing them over to me.

Since Adeline sent me a text, I assume she's got the number she never used for six months, but I don't want her to have any excuses. If I don't get a call today, I'll be back every day until Shaylene lets me through.

Why the hell would Adeline send me a text message and ghost me?

CHAPTER 2
ADELINE

I stare out the window of the teachers' lounge at the fancy Mercedes SUV. It's too tinted for me to say for certain, but I know in my gut it's Damon. I mindlessly rub my belly. I haven't blown up yet, but the bump is definitely noticeable. Which meant coming clean with my coworkers and principal two months ago. There's a good chance I won't see the end of the school year before this baby makes his or her arrival.

"Is he going to sit out there all day?" Isla says in her typical judgmental voice.

Thankfully, it's just her and our other teacher friend Sami in here with me, but soon more of the teachers will file in for lunch, and word will spread that Damon Siska is sitting in his car in our parking lot.

I'd rather chew glass than confess that he knocked me up after a one-night stand.

"How did he find me? Why is he here?" I mumble.

I've gotten his calls since the Chicago Grizzlies won the bowl last weekend. The first message was odd after having not spoken to him in six months. "Hey, call me." I assumed he might've been looking for a booty call, but what would a champion-winning running back need with me? Surely he has his pick of women.

I didn't respond because I doubted he was looking for a pregnant hook-up. From my experience with him, he's like a damn acrobat in bed, constantly changing positions, with the stamina of a superhero. No complaints from me. By the time my orgasm came, I saw stars from coming so hard.

His second, third, and fourth messages were much more forceful, and by his fifth, he said it was unfair for me to not answer his calls. I don't know what the heck he meant with that comment, but I do know I'm not ready to see him. Because that will mean coming clean about the situation I'm in. And though I've been psyching myself up to do so for months, it's going to change everything, and I don't know that I'm ready for that. Again.

When Elijah showed up at my classroom door yesterday with a note that said Damon was here, I almost passed out. I literally had to close my eyes from feeling lightheaded. This is coming to a head, I know it. Today, he's been out here for hours. Our security guard-slash-fan of his, Vic, informed me shortly after school started that Damon was here, and I have no doubt he'll be here when I leave. There's no place for me to hide.

"How did he find out?" Sami asks, chomping on her carrot stick. "I'm still in disbelief that the guy I slept with wasn't him and that you got pregnant by the real Damon Siska."

When we first met Damon last summer, Sami didn't believe it was him because she'd had a one-night stand with a guy she'd thought was Damon Siska from the Chicago Grizzlies. Turns out it was just a guy who kind of looked like him and liked to use that fact to his full advantage.

"I don't know." I shake my head, still staring out at the vehicle.

I can't lie and say I was thrilled when that stick turned up with two lines. I immediately threw up, and not because of morning sickness. All in all, I've had a great pregnancy. Ever since I first felt the little flutters in my belly, I've been growing more excited, if not nervous.

"I thought you went to Chicago and told him?" Sami continues. She's also reading her latest gossip blog on her phone when real drama is unfolding right here in front of her.

"Oh, she went to tell him," Isla says. The way she drops her feet from the chair she's resting them on, I know she's prepared to tell Sami the whole story, but thankfully, some other teachers come into the room.

Teachers like Henry. He smiles at me, his gaze dropping to my stomach. That's the way it is these days. Opening up the fridge, he takes out his prepared lunch, then he walks over to me, glaring out the window. "Still here, huh? Talk about making a spectacle. Every student is making bets on who it is and who they're here for."

The day I hooked up with Damon, all of

the teachers were at the Colts game in the city. I'm sure some noticed I disappeared midway through, but I don't think anyone realized it was with Damon, though Henry has alluded he did.

I smile, not offering Henry much else. Leaving the window, I stalk over to the table with Sami and Isla, no longer able to talk freely.

Sami pushes her veggie plate toward me. "You need to eat."

I nod. "I had a big breakfast."

"Liar." Isla pulls an apple out of her lunch bag.

I stare at the prepared salad I picked up from the grocery store on the way in today. It looks about as appetizing as a piece of cardboard. "I want a Reuben. Why do I want a Reuben? I've never eaten one in all my life."

"Go to Ira's Deli over on Forest Drive. The best Reubens," Lloyd says from across the lounge, then carries on with Henry about the Reuben in great detail.

Saliva pools in my mouth, and I know that nothing will satisfy me now until I get that damn Reuben. I pick up my phone to see when the deli closes, crossing my fingers they aren't one of those places only open for lunch.

"What do you think his plan is? Chase you down at your car?" Isla asks in a low voice.

"It's kind of hot that he's here, no?" Sami asks, finally putting down her phone.

"Hot? Seriously, come back down to reality." Isla wasn't a fan when I slept with Damon, and when I got pregnant, she did the whole "I told you so" crap she always does when I do something she doesn't approve of.

"Oh, come on. He clearly just found out, and he tried to get in yesterday but Shaylene denied him, so he's going to wait outside the school all day until she leaves. Definitely not that jackass Damon I slept with."

"You are aware his name probably wasn't Damon, right?" I ask, grabbing a piece of broccoli. I have to remember that the health of my baby is what matters at this point, not my cravings.

I've rehearsed telling him for months. First, when I first went to tell him I was pregnant—

before I abandoned that plan—and every day since, knowing telling him is the right thing to do. Still, his lifestyle isn't one I want my baby exposed to, and he doesn't need the bad press of having a baby mama. Damon's got a reputation, and from all the scouring I did online, he comes from a wealthy family on the East Coast who will probably think I got myself pregnant on purpose. All of this runs through my head every time I gather the courage to consider reaching out to him.

My gaze meets Henry's across the room. If I was going to make this colossal of a mistake, couldn't it have been with an average Joe like Henry?

"I'm not an idiot. I know his name wasn't really Damon," Sami says, but she blushes.

Part of me thinks Sami wishes what was happening to me was happening to her.

"I'll go out there and confront him," Isla whispers. "Because God knows Vic won't."

"No. I have to see him at some point. I just have about three hours before I do." I lean back in my seat. He has to have better things to do than sit in a middle school parking lot all day. "If I'm lucky, he'll get sidetracked by a hot blond."

They both stare at me.

"You have a better chance of Vic actually doing his job and telling him to get off school property." Isla looks over my shoulder. "Get an autograph yet?"

I don't have to turn around to know she's talking to Vic. He's been going gaga over this whole "Damon Siska in the house" thing. That's what he keeps saying, earning an award for telling the most people that Damon was here looking for me yesterday. Although I never told anyone else at work who the father is, I'm sure people have put two and two together. Especially if they think about the Colts game this past summer, where we all saw Damon and Cooper Rice, the Grizzlies' quarterback.

"No. But if he's out there when I'm on bus duty, I plan on it," Vic says.

Isla rolls her eyes. "He's as pathetic as Lloyd, just in a different way." She points at the man in question who's now at the table with Henry.

Sami gives me a look, as if asking what Isla's smoking.

We watch as Lloyd pours his soup out of his thermos and shoves his tie over his shoulder, slurping the soup into his mouth with the spoon that snaps to the top of the thermos.

"I'm not sure," Sami starts, but I slide out of my chair.

"I have to finish my lesson plans for to-morrow. I'll talk to you later." I abruptly stand, and all eyes are on me.

"I'll stop by your room and walk you out after," Isla says.

"I'll be okay. You guys have enough to do."

I walk out of the teachers' lounge before anyone can say anything else to me. I appreciate them all standing by my side, but this is something I should've done months ago.

Once I'm back in my classroom, I shut the door to keep everyone out, but it's time I admit to myself that Damon is here, which means whether I like it or not, we'll be part of each other's lives for the long haul.

My forehead falls to my desk. Whose life did I hijack to be in this position? Because this sure as heck isn't how I saw my life going.

CHAPTER 3
DAMON

The bell rings, and kids file out of the school from three different sets of doors. Buses line the one driveway while teachers direct the kids where to go, but none of them are listening. Some are laughing with their friends, and others have their heads buried in their phones.

I scour the masses for Adeline, but nothing. For the thousandth time, I glance at the picture the private investigator gave me. Her hair might be a little longer than I remember, but other than that, she looks the same—beautiful in a way that can swing from one end of the spectrum to the other. She can either appear like a Sunday morning girl next door with a "let's go grab a coffee and a Danish" vibe or a stunningly beautiful woman going out for Sunday brunch at the hottest new place.

A few teachers wearing safety vests are sprinkled through the crowd, directing the children and parent pick-up. None of them are Adeline, which is probably good because at least this way there will be fewer witnesses when I do approach her. I don't need this situation gossiped about until I figure out a few things—the first one being whether the baby is actually mine. Don't get me wrong, I don't think she's the type to try to trap me or lie about her baby's parentage, but she did wait six months to message me about the pregnancy and then immediately went MIA.

I thought word would get around about my car being outside and maybe she'd come out, but I suspected she might play a game of chicken to see who would bail first. So I made sure to park by her car so I wouldn't miss her.

It's four thirty, and the after-school rush is long gone when three women come out of the building, followed by two men. One of the guy's eyes swings to my car first. He can't see in because of my tinted windows. I remember the guy from the rooftop on the day I met Adeline. I don't recall his name, but I do remember his protective gaze on Adeline the whole time I chatted with her. His zeroed-in attention now confirms I've been the talk of the school, and the brunette sandwiched between her friends walking this way already knows I'm here.

She's five feet from her car when I step out of mine. "Adeline?"

She freezes as if I'm taking her by surprise when we both know I'm not.

The redhead I also remember from the rooftop whispers something in Adeline's ear while the shorter woman smiles at me. The two of them have a conversation, the redhead eventually storming off while the shorter one stays by Adeline's side.

"Go ahead, Sami. I'm fine." Her eyes meet mine.

I forgot how magnetic her eyes are. Their light blue is similar to mine, but hers contrast with her dark hair.

"I'm not far if you need me," Sami says and rubs Adeline's arm.

I round Adeline's car to her side after Sami rushes off, looking over her shoulder with every step. "Ade—"

She's quick to cut me off. "First off, I'm sorry." Her attention moves to her stomach, and my eyes follow.

There's the baby bump. If she was telling the truth, then a part of me is growing in there. My heartbeat increases with the fact that this is likely my new reality.

"Can we go somewhere and talk?" I ask, not wanting to push her. She looks like a frightened animal, ready to bolt.

She nods, appearing almost relieved that this moment has finally come. "How about Ira's Deli on Forest? You can follow me if you'd like."

"Nah, I'll drive," I say, turning and heading to my car.

"You can follow," she says to my retreating back.

I stop and turn to face her. "I'd rather go together." Standing at the back of my car, I notice some people peering our way.

"Why?" She frowns.

"Oh, I don't know, maybe because I've been trying to talk to you for days and now that I actually have you in front of me, I'm not going to let you out of my sight." I swing my keys around my finger.

She glances around the parking lot.

"I'm pretty sure everyone still sitting in their car watching us right now already knows that little bundle of joy in your stomach is mine, so I wouldn't worry what they'll think if you get in my car."

"They don't." She shakes her head, but it's clear she's annoyed that I can read her thoughts.

"Who do they think is the father?" My jaw clenches, though I'm not sure why.

She grabs her keys from her purse, then her car beeps, indicating it's locked. "Let's go."

"Perfect." I round the back of my car to the passenger side and open the door for her.

She slides in without a look my way but mumbles, "Thanks."

I scour the mostly empty parking lot to see a few cars with drivers watching us, one being the guy who looks as if he wants to rip off my head. It occurs to me then that she might not be single. I came here assuming she was, but I can't imagine a woman as beautiful as she is being single for long, even if she's pregnant. I don't think most men would be cool being with a woman who's pregnant with another man's baby, but maybe she found out late that she's pregnant, and that's why I'm just finding out. Shit, what if they're trying to hustle me for money? Damn, my dad is gonna murder me when he finds out I'm in this position.

I drive us to Ira's Deli, and the only conversation is her instructing me where to go. Ira's is small, but I can never be too safe. Being seen at the school was already enough of a risk. If someone sees me walking into the deli with a pregnant woman I can't explain, things could escalate.

"What do you want? I'll go buy the sandwiches, and we can go back to your place to eat."

"Um…" She worries her bottom lip.

"If not your place, a park, somewhere I have less of a chance of being recognized."

I see hurt in her eyes, but she masks it quickly, her hand going to the door handle. "I'll get the sandwiches. What do you like?"

I fish a fifty from my wallet and hand it

to her. "Just get me a roast beef with mayo, please."

She stares at the fifty and huffs, taking it from my hand. "Sure."

After exiting the SUV, she walks inside. I watch her order, pay, and wait alongside the counter, pulling out her cell phone. My phone rings over Bluetooth, and I groan, seeing my teammate Miles's name on my screen. I probably shouldn't answer right now, but I'm already full of anxiety and could use a friendly voice.

"Hey," I answer.

"Did you find her?" his girlfriend, Bryce, asks, and I roll my eyes.

"Where's Cavanaugh?" I squeeze the steering wheel.

"Here. So are Coop and Elle. You're on speakerphone."

"Is this an intervention or something?" I lean back in my seat. They're the only four people who know about this situation—mostly because when that text came through on one of the best nights of my life, I had to tell someone.

"Of course not," Miles says. "We're your

friends and are going to see you through this."

"One of you is a reporter," I mention, and I hear Bryce scoff.

"I told you I won't report about this, but if you do decide to talk about it with the press, I better get an exclusive."

"Yeah, you'll get the whole spread. Bachelor of the Year knocked up his one-night stand and ruined his life."

"Your life isn't ruined because of a baby," Ellery says. "You have more than enough money to support him or her. Hell, you can give them a nanny twenty-four, seven. Do you know how many babies I see born into families who love them so much but don't have the financial means to take care of them? If you put the time and effort into fatherhood, this could end up being the best part of your life."

I roll my eyes, though she has a point. Ellery's a doctor at an inner-city hospital, but I don't want to be lectured while I'm trying to figure out if the baby is mine. I definitely slept with Adeline, and although she didn't seem like the type to sleep around, she could've fooled me.

She and Bryce begin talking to each other when I don't respond, complaining about me.

"I would have come with you," Miles says.

What can I say? I have great friends. Miles, who I've known since college, would lie down in front of a truck for me, but this isn't their problem. It's mine.

Adeline accepts a bag from the worker and walks out of the deli.

"Gotta go." The line clicks right as she opens the door.

"There's a park about two blocks over. Should offer you the privacy you want," she says as she gets in.

Once again, she directs me where to go. Once we're parked, she hands me my sandwich. I don't even open mine to eat, while she practically inhales hers. She could give our O-line a run for their money.

She glances at me, covering her mouth as she chews. "You're not eating?"

I shrug. My appetite hasn't been what it usually is since the news. She puts down her sandwich.

"Don't stop on my account. Please, you're eating for two."

She wipes her mouth with a napkin. "My salad at lunch didn't really cut it."

"You had a salad? Hate to break it to you, but if you're really growing half of me in that belly, a leafy bowl of vegetables isn't gonna cut it."

"You're telling me. I've never eaten this much in my life." With a small smile, she picks up the sandwich, not embarrassed that she can't stop eating it. I like it.

I chuckle. It's cute as fuck that she doesn't care what she looks like in front of me. I wait for her to finish eating before broaching the pink elephant wearing a glittery dress and high heels in the room.

Once she's done eating, she takes a water bottle out of her bag and sips it. "Man, I had no idea that all this time I was missing out by never eating a Reuben. Have you had one before?"

Are we seriously going to talk about Reubens?

"I think I had one once. Not a huge fan of rye bread."

She nods, and my G-Wagon fills with silence once more. She fiddles with her hands in her lap. We both turn to one another and start speaking at the same time, only to stop. I gesture for her to go.

"How did you find out?" she asks.

I tilt my head and frown, staring at her and trying to see something in her eyes that says she's joking, but she only looks concerned. "Did you not want me to know?"

She shakes her head. "I went to Chicago to tell you once." There's a note of… something in her voice. Displeasure? Disappointment?

"What? When? I'm pretty sure I would've remembered being told I'm going to be a father."

She looks out the window for a second. "You were with someone. I didn't want to interrupt."

I shake my head. "I'm so confused. Adeline, you sent me a text message right after the Grizzlies won the championship, telling me you were pregnant."

Her head whips in my direction, her eyes wide. "No, I didn't."

I fish out my phone from the center console and pull up the text message I've read a hundred times since I received it. I turn my screen to show her, and she shakes her head, confusion coating her features.

"Are you sure it's not another Adeline? I never sent that message."

I cough a laugh. "Are you insinuating that I knocked up two women named Adeline?"

She lifts her shoulders, then bends to retrieve her bag, digging for her cell phone. "I'm not sure, because I'll show you I never sent you that message. And I know for a fact because every day I pull up your contact to send you a message and lose the nerve. I didn't want to ruin your season, and after you won, I figured it was worse for me to tell you while you were probably celebrating and so happy. I was waiting for things to calm down a little."

She pulls out her phone and shows me the message exchanges under my name on her phone. And it only contains the messages I've sent to her in the past few days.

It doesn't matter to me whether she sent the message or didn't. There's only one question to ask at this point. "Adeline, is the baby mine?"

CHAPTER 4
ADELINE

"Y es." My shoulders sag, and I brace myself for his reaction, my stomach tightening.

Damon blows out a breath, his large hands flexing over the steering wheel until his knuckles turn white, then he spreads them wide open. The man has beautiful hands. Long, lean fingers and perfectly trimmed nails.

"Really?" I open my mouth to answer, but he shakes his head before I can. "Don't answer that."

I've had six months to get comfortable with the fact that I'm going to have a baby out of wedlock with a man who picks up a different woman every night of the week. At first, I thought, why couldn't I get knocked up by a guy like Miles Cavanaugh or Cooper Rice if it had to be a football player? But only Damon is the one who causes my heart to beat uncontrollably every time I see him. Even after our one-night stand, every time I saw him on TV or pulled up an image on the computer, I had the same physical reaction. Sitting next to him now, I feel the same way.

I wait and give him time to wrap his head around the news.

"To hear it… it makes it real, you know?" His normally upbeat and playful voice is low and rough.

"Funny, the kicking made it real for me." I give him a wan smile.

He stares at my stomach protruding from my open jacket. I place my hand over the swell as if I'm protecting our little bean.

His lips thin, and he inhales a deep breath. "Hopefully you won't fault me for wanting a paternity test."

I shake my head. "Of course not. I have a doctor's appointment next week. I'll gladly ask how we go about getting one." I knew the day he found out, a paternity test would be a priority. I'm sure I'm not the first woman to tell him he's going to be a father.

"It's not that I don't think… I mean, you don't seem like the type… or at least you didn't seem to be."

"Someone who would lie about something like that?" I arch an eyebrow.

He can't really say I'm not the type of woman to sleep with a virtual stranger because that's exactly what I did. Even if it was the first and last time.

"Yeah." He nods.

Silence descends on us once again, and I decide that I need to break it and explain myself. I'm the only one in the world who knows he is definitely the father of this baby, unless there's such a thing as immaculate conception.

I turn in my seat to face him, although he's looking out his windshield toward the woods. "I should have tried harder to tell you, and I'm sorry for that. I've had all this time to prepare for the baby, and you haven't. That's not fair. Early on, I went to your apartment. Took the train down and an Uber over there, but when my car pulled up to the curb across from your building, you were outside with Miles and Cooper and a couple other women. I recognized the one from the day we met. I was hoping to approach you alone, but I didn't have a choice. While I was gathering my courage, another car double-parked, and you went over to open the door. This woman with an amazing body in a small bikini and a see-through cover-up practically jumped into your arms. Your hands were…" I shake my head, not needing to discuss all the insecurities in my head at the moment. Especially since I was nauseated and felt like a slob from all the changes my body was going through.

His head rocks back as if he remembers exactly who and when I mean. I'm surprised, honestly. The rumors about him suggest she'd be one of a long line of girls to grace his bed.

"Anyway, you guys filed into the SUV and took off. I told myself I'd come back another day, but the Grizzlies kept getting closer to the championship. You were playing so great. I didn't want to mess with your head and have you blame this little one for ruining your chance to win the championship. I promised myself I'd wait until the season was over, then tell you." I press my lips together, nervous for his reaction.

His forehead wrinkles. "But you didn't send the text?"

"No. I mean, I watched the championship, saw you and the other captains accepting the trophy, Miles's declaration to Bryce on stage, but I would never have told you over a text. So when you started texting me out of the blue, asking me questions, and giving away that you knew about the pregnancy, I didn't understand. I was scared."

I thought Damon was the type of guy who doesn't think about his words, just spits them out as soon as the thoughts form, but again, the vehicle is quiet while he seems to assess everything I said. Guess now it's my turn to stare at the woods.

"Thank you."

I look at him from the corner of my eye. Why the heck is he thanking me? "Sorry?"

"You're right. My season would've gone to shit. I'm not sure I love that you kept it from me, but my head would've been all over the place." His gaze goes to my stomach. "I want you to know if the baby is mine,

I take care of my responsibilities. I'm not going to just leave you or send you a check. I'll help you raise the baby."

I didn't know how he was going to feel about this. Whether he'd try to throw cash at me to keep me quiet and make me go away. The more the baby grew in my stomach, the more I hoped that he would step up. I want my baby to have a father in his or her life.

"Well, first things first. Let's get the paternity test, then we can go from there," I say.

He gets a sour look on his face. "I don't think you're lying, but my dad will kill me if I don't get one done. Once we get the paternity test back, we'll need to talk about a few things."

"I don't want anything from you, Damon."

His fair eyebrows rise to his hairline. "You want to raise the baby by yourself?"

His jaw clenches, and if I'm honest, his reaction to this entire situation surprises me. Of course the funny good-time guy isn't here, but he so quickly seems... invested. Maybe I should have expected it, but I didn't.

"I just meant I won't be looking for money or anything."

He starts the vehicle and puts his seat belt on, eyeing me to do the same.

"We're done?" I ask.

"We can't really have this conversation until after we find out about the paternity. Then we can make some arrangements."

"Is there something I should be concerned about?" I'm not sure what he means by arrangements.

He finishes backing out of the spot and puts his hand over my clasped ones in my lap. "Of course not. When did you say your doctor's appointment is?"

"Next Tuesday," I answer.

"Where should I pick you up?" He removes his hand, and I miss the feel of them immediately.

"I can drive myself."

He thinks about it for a second while driving back to the school. "Fine."

Once we reach the school, I give him the doctor's address and the time of my appointment. He thanks me. Now this entire exchange feels more awkward and weird than when it started.

"Is there anything you need before Tuesday?" he asks as I place my hand on the door handle to get out.

"No, I'm fine." I open the door but stop from exiting and turn to him. "Please know, I'm not your worry, just baby."

He scrunches up his forehead. "The baby is inside of *you*, so as of right now, you're both my worry. Call me if you need anything."

"I will. Thank you, Damon. Thanks for understanding. Some men would have been upset with me for waiting so long." Even though I didn't actually instigate this meeting. Note to self: find out who sent that text.

"We're in this together." He smiles for the first time all day, and it causes my stomach to flutter. Damn him and his charm.

I nod and exit the car. He waits for me to get into my car and doesn't pull out until I do. He's taking this whole protective thing a little too seriously, but damn if it doesn't give me a warm feeling in my chest.

———

I pull into my parents' driveway and walk into their house. The house smells like chili, and my mouth waters even though I just had that Reuben sandwich. "Mom? Dad?"

My mom comes out of the kitchen archway, wiping her hands on a dish towel. She was the first person I told about the pregnancy. It wasn't like she could get angry. I'm twenty-nine years old, with a job and a house of my own. Her worry has been mostly contained to who the father is and what that might mean for the baby and myself.

"Just in time, the cornbread is out of the oven." She hugs me and places her hand on my stomach. "How are my two girls?"

"You have no idea if it's a girl," I say, following her into the kitchen.

"Sure, I do. It's the way you're carrying her. A mother knows these things." She taps her temple.

"Because you had so many kids of your own?" I take a piece of the cornbread she's cutting and quirk an eyebrow at her since I'm an only child.

She points at me. "You just wait and see."

I'm not sure when to drop the bomb about Damon visiting me at school. It'll probably freak her out.

My dad walks in and leans in to kiss my cheek. "Look who's here. How's my grandbaby?"

I run my hand down my belly. "He or she is good. Kicking like crazy and making me eat about five thousand calories a day. Have you been to Ira's Deli before?"

My dad nods because he's been everywhere. The minute a new restaurant opens, he's the first one in line. Maybe I'm just a foodie like him, and it's not the baby at all.

"The Reuben is so good." I lick my lips for emphasis.

"Since when do you eat Reubens?" My mom looks up from spooning the chili into our bowls on the counter.

"Since this little one." I pat my swollen belly.

"Speaking of which, Isla and Sami messaged to ask if we're having a baby shower. I didn't want to tell them you were adamant we don't tell any family members. I just said I'd discuss it with you. You know Aunt Claudia and Grandma Hilda will be upset when they find out we've hidden it from them all these months."

I sigh. "Well, that might change now." I pick at my piece of cornbread. "Damon stopped by the school today. Apparently he received a text about my… situation."

"Siska?" my dad practically shouts.

"Do we know another Damon?" I ask.

He laughs. "Well, technically, I don't know a Siska." He shrugs, putting cheese and sour cream into his chili and taking it to the table.

"You will. You both will."

My mom's smile vanishes, and she concentrates on cutting the rest of the cornbread. She's worried about what all this will mean when it's public knowledge that Damon is having a baby.

"Mom," I say, placing my hand on her arm.

"I know he's the father and should be involved. I just don't want you to be dragged through the mud in those damn gossip blogs and magazines. You know people will say you trapped him or something."

My mom has always been the one to

speak my fears out loud. I'm not sure if it's because we're close or if she's just so communicative, but she always knows what's running through my head.

"We'll see. He wants a paternity test," I admit before chomping down on the piece of cornbread, grabbing my bowl of chili, and going to the table.

"We knew he would," my dad says.

"That fool thinks it's not his? Who does he think my daughter is?" Mom shakes her head.

Dad looks up from his chili, smirking. That's my mom, always protective over us.

"Darling, he's a professional football player. Do you know how many women have probably accused him of fathering their babies?" He winks at me.

"Because he's a manwhore. How about he keeps it in his pants, and maybe then not so many women can accuse him?" She's getting worked up.

"Mom, just come over and eat."

She brings her bowl of chili and a plate of cornbread to the table. "You can't trust him. I've been Googling him," she says, whispering the word Google.

I searched him too. Most of what came up was a million pictures of him with different women he's dated or slept with, from celebrities to influencers to doctors to regular women. How is it that me, a regular middle school teacher, gets gifted with his baby?

"Let's just see what happens, okay? And you have to be on your best behavior because he's going to be at the doctor's appointment on Tuesday." I point my spoon at her for emphasis.

"Oh man, I hope the doctor hides all her sharp instruments." My dad shakes his head, laughing at his own joke.

"Mom?" I ask with my eyebrows raised.

She holds up her hands. "I'm a grown woman. I can handle my temper."

Dad buries his head in his meal because we both know my mom is unable to hide her mama bear instincts when it comes to protecting her cub.

CHAPTER 5
DAMON

I arrive early to the doctor's office, pulling my hat low on my head to hopefully not be recognized. I intend to ask the doctor for after-hours appointments after this first one, but I didn't want to put that on Adeline so soon or put a spotlight on how much her life might change when this gets out.

Instead of walking into the office and sitting in a waiting room full of women trying to figure out who I am, I loiter around the hallway outside.

The elevator dings, and Adeline steps out with another woman. The woman is older but just as tall as Adeline and bears the same dark hair, except it's much shorter. Where Adeline's face is rounder, her mother's is more oval. But that's about the only difference between the duo.

Adeline smiles, and it's so genuine my heart hurts. I've had no sleep since she confirmed the news. I'm not sure I'm father material, and I really hope she doesn't think I'm relationship material. Sure, I gave her my number last August, but that was only because I wanted her in my bed a second time.

"Damon, this is my mother, Marge." Adeline holds her hand out to the woman who has an expression similar to what a guard dog might give an intruder. Her teeth aren't showing or anything, but it's clear she's not happy with me or this entire situation. "She's been coming to my appointments up until now."

I would've been too, if Adeline had told me. After I left her last week and rolled over our conversation on the drive home, it was apparent to me that thanking her for not telling me about the pregnancy before now was probably a dick move. I should've wanted to know about my kid from the start. I should've wanted to read books on pregnancy. I should have wanted to be here, holding her hand for every appointment.

I hold my hand out to Marge. "Nice to meet you."

She shakes my hand. "You as well."

I worry that I'm already down by fifty points, and there's two minutes left in the fourth quarter as far as she's concerned. Plus, it doesn't take much for people to find out about my reputation as a professional football player who doesn't do relationships. I wouldn't want that for my little girl either.

"Okay, well, let's go in." Adeline opens the door to the doctor's office.

My eyes instantly scan the room. Only two other women are waiting. One has her head buried in an e-reader and the other in a magazine. Neither even look up when we enter.

Marge sits in a chair on the farthest side of the room by the window, crosses her legs, and stares at me. Good to know where we stand.

"I don't think your mom likes me," I whisper to Adeline when we reach the counter.

She tells the receptionist her name and hands her a credit card from her wallet.

The receptionist squints as if she's trying to place me. Fuck, I'm going to need a shit-ton of NDAs. My dad's going to be pissed I didn't dole them out before walking my ass in here.

"My mom doesn't know you," Adeline says.

"Her scowl says she knows *of* me."

Adeline laughs, accepts her credit card back from the woman, and folds a piece of paper into threes while the woman tells us the doctor is running behind.

On our way back over to her mom, I lean in close. "How much?"

"How much what?" She puts the paper in her purse.

"How much has this cost you so far?"

"I have insurance." She sits next to her mom, and I realize then that Marge took the seat in the middle of three vacant seats. My only option is to sit on the other side, next to her mom. "She said the doctor is running a few minutes late."

I hate the fact she's telling her mom that, and I'm right here. I don't want to be a dick.

I understand her mom has been here for the last six months and I haven't, but it's not because I didn't want to be. I have a list of questions I want answered by either Adeline or the doctor, and her mom's attitude toward me isn't making this any easier.

"Marge, will you be coming in with us as well?" I ask, although I can guess the answer.

She looks at Adeline, who looks at me as though I've offended someone.

Holding up both hands, I say, "I didn't know if there was a condition on how many could be in the room."

"No. It's fine for all three of us," Adeline answers.

"So, Damon, how long of a trip was it out here for you this morning?" Marge asks.

"Not long." I'm lying through my teeth, and she knows it. Chicago traffic is brutal. Although I thought the commute out of town wouldn't be a problem, I was wrong. Seems both going in or out of the city is a nightmare to navigate in the morning.

"Oh, well that's good." Her tone doesn't make it sound as though it's good.

I sit in the chair, my elbows resting on

my knees, waiting for Adeline's name to be called because I can't handle this threesome anymore.

The two other women waiting are called in by the nurses, and I relax a little.

"Must be hard," Marge says, obviously seeing my visible relief at their absence.

"I just don't want news to spread, you know?"

"Oh, I meant trying to figure out if you've knocked them up too."

"Mom!" Adeline screeches.

I laugh. I can't help it. There aren't a lot of people ballsy enough to say something like that to someone's face. Other than myself, of course. "Someone's been reading up on me, I see?"

Marge turns to me, her back to Adeline. "It didn't take but a few keystrokes. You like your women, from what I've read."

So I was right, this is where her disdain is coming from. My reputation for being a playboy. I'd hate to inform Marge that her daughter was a willing participant the night we were together, and she knew the score.

"Mom, we've been over this." Adeline glances at the receptionist. "We weren't in a relationship. It was a one-night stand," she whispers.

Marge holds her hand up to her daughter and faces me directly. "I understand the benefits you have, being in the profession you're in, but now there are responsibilities for you to step up for, and I'm sorry if I worry that when this little one comes, I'll be the only one holding my daughter's hand."

I take off my hat, running my hands through my hair. The gasp from the receptionist confirms I've given myself away. All of our eyes land on her, and she quickly turns her attention to her computer. Fuck, I should have listened to my dad's voice in my head. ND fucking As.

I clear my throat. "I understand you're worried. I'm well aware of my reputation, but as I informed Adeline last week, I don't walk away from my responsibilities. I'm here today, and I plan on being at every appointment from this moment forward, including the birth. I understand you might not take my word for it, but just like my high school coach who said I wasn't fast enough to play wide receiver, I'll prove you wrong."

"Um, the birth thing..." Adeline's expression suggests we might have to talk about that.

I lean forward past her mom so I can meet her gaze. "Don't worry, I'll stay by your head."

"Adeline," the nurse calls, and our conversation ends.

Adeline stands, grabs her purse from the floor, and walks to the nurse at the open door. I wait for Marge, but she stops and smiles at me, squeezing my hand. I'm assuming that's a good sign, although I don't have a lot of experience with parents. Other than Greta's, but I'd known them my entire life.

The nurse takes us into an exam room, then leaves with Adeline.

"Where are they going?" I ask, rising from my chair next to Marge.

"Just to weigh her. Make sure she isn't gaining too much weight." She laughs at my confused expression and pats my knee. "Relax, she's been great."

"Aren't pregnant women allowed to eat

whatever they want? It's like open season for them to eat all the food they want?"

"That's not Adeline. She'd never do that. I don't say this badly, but you really don't know one another, so I'll clue you in. My daughter follows the rules. She's not going to gain more than the thirty pounds she's supposed to. She's going to continue walking until the day she delivers, get all the sleep she needs, and she's religious about taking her prenatal vitamins. I know you didn't choose this, but you couldn't have picked a better woman to carry your baby."

I can't respond because Adeline returns with the nurse. She slides up on the exam table with the paper sheet, and the nurse goes behind the computer, scanning her card to access her files.

"Adeline, your weight is still great. I'm going to take your blood pressure now."

The nurse does everything she needs to, praising Adeline with everything she checks.

"Thanks," Adeline says, and the nurse tells us that the doctor will be in soon.

I stand, unable to sit any longer, and I take off my hat because I find them uncomfortable. Posters on the walls show the different stages of pregnancy and how big the baby is.

"The baby is the size of an ear of corn," I say out loud, though it's really meant more for myself.

"Crazy, right?" Adeline runs her hands over her stomach. She's wearing jeans and a sweater today, her dark hair curled into waves, and her makeup is natural, with cheeks so rosy I don't know if it's from the cold air outside or makeup.

A knock lands on the door, and we all say, "Come in" at once and laugh.

The doctor walks in and stops when she sees me. "I heard a rumor that we had someone new joining us." She smiles at me, then nods to Adeline's mom. "How are you, Marge?"

"I think I'm about to be replaced," she says, but her lips turn up in a smile.

"I'm Doctor Griffin." She holds her hand out in front of me.

"Damon Siska," I say.

"I know. I'm a big fan." She sits on the round stool and looks us all over. "So, anything new?"

Adeline laughs. "Damon is the... well, one thing we need to talk to you about today is a paternity test."

"Okay." She doesn't react at all, giving no indication as to whether she finds this to be an odd request or not. She simply scans her keycard at the computer and types something in. "It's not dangerous anymore like it was in the past. You have the easy part, Damon, just a swab in your cheek. And now with noninvasive testing, we'll take some blood from you, Adeline, and the test will come back in about a week or less."

"Easy then. Good." I don't know if it's nerves or trepidation coursing through my veins.

She types some more in the computer, then stands and washes her hands. "Ready for the exam?"

Adeline lies down, seeming to know the drill.

"Do you want me to, um... leave?" I ask Adeline.

She shakes her head. "It's nothing you haven't seen before."

I have no idea if she's serious or not, which goes back to the fact that I don't know her well enough yet. Marge laughs, signaling to me that her daughter was joking.

"We're not going to look vaginally anyway," Dr. Griffin says. "She's playing with you."

"Hell, I didn't know. I'm usually the jokester, but I'm finding myself off my game with this newfound situation." I walk over.

Adeline holds out her hand to me as though it's second nature. I slide my hand into hers, and she squeezes. "I know you're uncomfortable, and it's taking a lot to be here, but I do appreciate it. I had to lighten up this room. It's way too serious in here."

"Thanks," I say, smiling at her and remembering why I was attracted to her in the first place, besides her killer looks.

Dr. Griffin lifts Adeline's shirt, exposing her belly. I look down at her, wondering if this is okay, but Adeline smiles at me.

"Since we just did an ultrasound last month, we'll hear the heart rate and make sure it's strong."

"Did you find out the sex?" I ask.

Adeline shakes her head. "Do you want to know?"

I have no idea what to say. "It's up to you." That feels like the right thing.

"I'd like it to be a surprise," she says. "If you don't mind."

"Not at all."

Marge comes to the other side of the table, and I assume this will be us on delivery day too. Dr. Griffin feels around Adeline's stomach, places some gel on it, then places a little wand-type thing on her belly, moving it around until the sound of a rapid heartbeat echoes through the room.

My body goes limp, and I stare at her stomach in awe. "Is that…"

Adeline's eyes swim with unshed tears.

"Our baby," I say, and she nods.

Holy shit, this all got really real, really quick.

CHAPTER 6
ADELINE

Dr. Griffin called and asked if Damon and I could come in and meet with her. The paternity test is back, and I worry why she didn't just tell me the results over the phone. I mean, I *know* Damon is the father. But he was more than willing to drive back out here. Since it's his offseason, he said other than some sponsorships and volunteer work, his schedule is free.

Damon's Mercedes is parked in the lot when I pull in. Luckily, Dr. Griffin asked us to come in after hours, so I'm not missing any more work. I park my little domestic sedan next to his fancy car, and he climbs out immediately.

"How was your day?" he asks.

The truth is, we haven't really spoken much or gotten to know one another any better than before he found out I was pregnant. This is the first time he's asked about me personally and not just about my health. Progress, I suppose. Not that I want a relationship with the infamous Damon Siska, but if we're going to be coparents, I'd like to know the man I'm sending my child off to every other weekend.

"It was okay."

I don't bother going into the fact that since he showed up at the school, he's been the only thing people talk about. If I thought rumors were bad when I was a middle schooler, it's nothing like now. But this town and my school community are filled with good people because I haven't seen anything in the press about it yet, thank God. Though I have no doubt it's coming at some point.

"I can't imagine teaching hormone-crazed pre-teens all day." He opens the door to the doctor's office building.

"Thanks."

When we reach the elevator, he presses the button, and it's there immediately because most of the offices in the building are probably closed already. We step in, and once we're in the enclosed space, all I can smell is his cologne.

Did he put that on just to come to the doctor's appointment?

Maybe he has a hot date after he leaves here.

Ugh, why does that thought bother me so much?

"So…" he says when I don't respond to his question because I'm busy fixating on who he might be hooking up with tonight.

"Oh, um… the boys are the worst. Always picking on the girls because they think they're flirting. And the way the girls flirt back as if they like to be treated that way. It's really sad."

We reach our floor, and he holds out his hand for me to go first. "It really comes down to the boys and their egos. They don't want them crushed, so the only way they can get a girl to talk to them is to pick on them. Don't hold it against them too much. Eventually, boys like them turn into men like me after they find their confidence."

I stop at the door to the doctor's office and raise my eyebrows, then shift my vision down to my stomach.

He laughs and moves his hand to run it through his hair, but stops since it's gelled and perfectly in place. Again, the fact he probably put in all this effort because he has a date overtakes all my other thoughts. "Okay, you got me there. But everybody has to start somewhere."

I reach for the doorknob, but he moves in front of me and tugs at the handle, opening it to let me in first.

"I never realized you were such a gentleman."

He laughs again, but this time it's a deep chuckle that radiates into my bones. "We really should play a game of get-to-know-each-other. Then again, if your mom invites me to dinner, I'll get all the answers I need."

My face heats, and I swallow hard. "What did she tell you? You were alone with her for, like, two minutes while they weighed me." I'm going to have to talk to my mom about this.

"She just said that you're a rule-follower. It did make me wonder how far we're talking. Like two below the speed limit kinda thing?"

We're in the office, and I stare blankly at him. "I'm not that bad."

"Well, I can't guarantee what that little one will be like. I'm the biggest rule-breaker I know, so we might have a little hellion on our hands."

I run my hands over my belly as though I'm being protective, and he shakes his head. "Maybe nurture will win out."

"I have some strong genes," he says and eyes someone over my shoulder.

I hate the way my heart pitter-patters when he refers to the baby as his when the paternity hasn't been defined yet. I mean, the baby *is* his, but he has every right to want to wait until science confirms it.

"Hey, you two," Dr. Griffin says, coming to the open window at the receptionist area. "Come on, I'll let you in."

Damon puts his hand on the small of my back, and goosebumps chase up my spine. Nope, my body cannot react to his touch. He'll be in my life for the rest of time now, and things need to remain uncomplicated. I can't strive to have a relationship with a guy like him. Beyond the obvious complications if things didn't work out, dating a man who plays professional football can't be easy. The women and the press would be like a tsunami to my self-esteem.

Dr. Griffin wears her white coat over a pair of scrubs. "Sorry about my attire, emergency delivery."

"No problem. I'm just happy you were able to see us after hours," Damon says.

She walks us to her office instead of an exam room and tells us to take the two seats in front of her desk. Now I'm scared. Maybe something more than just who the father is came back? Do they look at more than paternity in these tests?

When she looks directly at Damon, my stomach churns. This is the moment.

"I got your lawyer's NDA, Damon," Dr. Griffin says. "My entire staff has signed them, and we've sent them back over, but I wanted to assure you that I cannot and would not share anything about you two anyway. My staff knows the rules as well. So please feel safe here, and from this point, we

can definitely do before- or after-hours appointments."

The perks of being a famous pro athlete.

"Thank you, I appreciate it and hope it
wasn't too much trouble." Damon glances at
me. "The press will be all over this, and I'd
rather not put Adeline through that during
the pregnancy."

Dr. Griffin smiles. "That's very nice of
you, and it makes me happy since I get to
say congratulations to you."

My attention focuses on Damon to judge
his reaction.

He turns to stare at my stomach, inhales
deeply, and smiles. It isn't a forced smile, but
a real, true smile that meets his eyes. And
damn it all to hell, that smile brands my
heart. Even though he's only had a short
time to soak this information in, he's happy
that he'll be a father.

She hands the papers to each of us and
leans back in her seat, watching our re-
actions.

Damon's hand reaches toward me, but
he retracts it. "There's a lot we'll have to
figure out now."

Ever since he showed up at my school,

I've wondered where the smart-mouthed, flirtatious version of Damon Siska is, because he's all business with me. I'm sure his lawyer will have papers for me to sign. My stomach tightens, and my heart falters for a beat. How did I never consider the fact that he's got more money and resources than me?

Oh god, I need to get my own lawyer.

"Let's set up your next appointment. I know you didn't get to see the ultrasound, Damon. Would you like to do another one? There would be a cost involved."

"Cost is no problem. I'd love to." Damon sits on the edge of his seat, probably ready to throw out some credit card with no spending limit.

"Are you okay with that, Adeline?" Dr. Griffin asks me. What does she expect me to say now that she's already put it out there?

"Sure."

Damon smiles at me.

"Also, I know you discussed with Adeline that she doesn't want to know the sex of the baby, but if you do want to know, Damon, I can tell you."

Damon shakes his head. "No. We'll wait.

I like the idea of it being a surprise." He smiles at me again.

I force one of my own. This is all slipping out of my control. For the past six months, I've been the one who decided everything. Now that it's confirmed he's the father, I realize he has as much say in things as I do.

We make our next appointment, and Dr. Griffin walks us out of her office, down the vacant hallway, and through the quiet waiting room.

"Thank you," Damon says, putting out his hand.

"You're welcome. Congratulations again. I know you two have a lot to figure out, but I have a feeling it will all work out." She winks in my direction.

I want to shake my head and say I don't need us to be a family. I mean, we will be our own version of a family, but not one where Damon and I share the same bed.

Although he is skilled in that department. More skilled than anyone else I've ever been with. By a mile.

We say goodbye and walk over to the elevator, ride down to the cars, and stand behind his vehicle for a moment.

"You're okay with the news?" I ask.

He shrugs. "I already figured."

"Because I'm not the type who sleeps around?" I doubt he means it as an insult, but I'm taking it as one. Just because I'm not like that girl who threw herself in his arms wearing nothing but a string bikini and a cover-up that day, who says I couldn't have found another guy to sleep with me that month?

"You're taking offense to that?" His eyebrows raise.

"No, but I'm not some single crazy cat lady who knits on Friday nights and cries into her ice cream bowl on Saturdays."

Okay, slow down, hormones, we're veering off the track.

He laughs, and it echoes in the mostly empty parking lot. "Damn, I might have to spy on you now to make sure." I roll my eyes, and his laugh sobers. "I just meant you're different, and I knew it when we met. You weren't hooking up with me because of who I was."

I put a hand on my hip. "Then why did I hook up with you?"

He bites his bottom lip, and electricity

shoots between my legs, leaving an enjoyable buzzing sensation behind. Yeah, he was good at that too. Bastard.

"My charm won you over."

I hate that he's right. The full sleeve of tattoos on both arms that were on display that day didn't hurt either. The fact that he was Damon Siska, professional football player, was actually a turn-off, but it was clear how he'd charmed his way into a long line of panties.

"I'm right, aren't I?" he asks when I don't say anything.

"I don't think that ego of yours needs any more petting."

He covers his heart with his hand as if I've shot an arrow at him. "I'm the father of your baby. How can you say such hurtful things?"

"Oh please, you're going to use that after officially knowing for what? Twenty minutes?"

He stuffs his hands into his coat pockets. I'm also growing colder the longer we stand out here.

"Do you need anything?" he asks, and I

shake my head. "Money? I want to pay the doctor's bills."

"Nope. I have insurance."

"The baby can go on my insurance after they're born."

"We should probably set a time to talk this stuff over." I don't want to do it now. I need to find my own lawyer.

"Definitely. Um… I haven't told my family yet. I wanted to wait for the test result on the off chance I was wrong about you. My dad… I'm not sure how much you know about me, but my dad will want to get lawyers involved, papers drawn up." He stares at the ground and rocks back on his feet.

"Of course," I say, fear-stricken.

He lifts his gaze, and there's something there I can't read, but he takes my hands. "Oh, you're cold. You need to get in the car."

"I'm fine." Except for the fact I want to get in my car and drive far, far away from here before he can try to take my baby.

"I will protect you and the baby. I won't let him bulldoze you into signing anything you don't want."

Naively, maybe, I trust his words and

smile at him. "Okay," I say, hoping like hell my trust isn't thrown back in my face.

"Now, go get in your car. I'll be in touch. If you need anything before then, let me know." He opens my car door, and once I'm in, he eyes the seat belt. "Buckle up."

I nod.

"Good night, Damon."

"Good night, Adeline."

He shuts my door and climbs into his fancy G-Wagon.

Could I have been wrong about him? Is Damon Siska really a good guy under the macho playboy act?

CHAPTER 7

DAMON

'm going to be a dad.

The thought cycles in my brain over and over on the drive home. I tried to save face in front of Adeline and make her believe I'm totally cool with this new role so she wouldn't worry, but damn, I'm filled with fucking fear. Then, like an idiot, I brought up my dad and all the lawyer shit he's surely going to throw at me… her… us. Why would I worry her like that? I shouldn't even tell my family, any of them.

I pull into my designated parking spot in the garage across from my apartment building. Instead of heading to my apartment, I go into Peeper's Alley, the bar at the bottom level of the four-flat, needing something to drink. When I approach, I tear down the poster board someone hand wrote "The Den" on and put it up on the gate to the stairs that lead to the three apartments above. Over the years, this place has come to be known by the moniker because of all the Grizzlies who have lived here.

"Damon," Ruby says from behind the bar when I enter the dated establishment. She hands a pint of beer to one of her many male customers who line the stools day and night.

She's opted not to make this bar trendy like the rest of the area. Instead, she refuses to serve anything other than beer and hard alcohol. Ruby is always lecturing any woman who comes in and asks for a seltzer, telling them they need to learn how to order a real drink. She's a little rough around the edges, but she treats me and the other two Grizzlies players who live in the building like her sons.

"Hey, Rubes, a shot of tequila and a beer."

She nods, and I wait. I have a tab here that she charges every month. I down the shot right after she finishes pouring it and wait for her to fill my pint of beer.

"Your crew is in the private room." She nods toward the room in the back.

Let's just say this place has become a popular hangout for women who hope to find us here, so the private room allows us privacy when we don't want to deal with any of that shit.

"Thanks." I pick up my beer and raise it in cheers.

The moment I walk into the private room, I change my mind and wish I would've gone up to my apartment. Bryce is cozy in Miles's lap while Cooper and Ellery sit with barely any space between them. It's like being the fifth wheel, and all I have to contribute is a pregnant one-night stand.

All four of them look up at me when I open the door.

"Daddy's home!" Cooper calls.

"Shut the fuck up." I look behind me, worried someone might have heard.

"Oh, come on. Most of them can't even hear what the person next to them is saying." Ellery sticks up for her supposed "best friend." She swears she doesn't want to fuck

Cooper and he swears the same, but they're delusional.

I don't know how they've gone this long ignoring the pull between them. Not pressing Adeline's back against the cool metal of the elevator wall and kissing the shit out of her earlier was pure torture. She's somehow even hotter now that she's carrying my child.

I really hope this infatuation I have with her is because she's carrying my baby. Like some kind of caveman reaction. Because every night since I found out, I've beat off to images of her riding me with her swollen belly and big tits. It's pathetic really, and I need to get laid.

"You're crabby," Bryce says, pushing her finger into my bicep as I sit between Miles and Cooper.

Horny is more accurate.

"So?" Miles asks, the one friend in this room who isn't afraid to dive straight into the serious shit.

I nod and sip my beer.

"Congratulations." Cooper pats my back, and I cough on my beer.

"I'm going to get a round of shots. Damon's gonna be a daddy." Ellery rounds her chair and heads into the bar area before I can stop her. "Rubes, a round of shots for us," I hear her call.

"Are you upset?" Bryce asks.

"No."

"Scared?" Miles asks.

"Shitless." I sip my beer again but continue swallowing until I finish the fucking thing. I slide the empty glass on the wooden table and rock my head back.

"Are you going to marry her?" Cooper asks.

I whip my head over to him. "Have you fucked Ellery yet?"

His head rears back, and he honestly looks confused as to why I'd ask him that question. Because Cooper fucking Ellery is in the same realm of possibility as pigs flying or hell freezing over. The man cannot make a move to save his life, and I'm no different when it comes to commitment.

"No, I'm not going to marry her," I answer before Cooper says anything.

"Are you going to tell your parents?" Miles asks.

Silence fills the room. I'm going to disappoint my dad. Everyone knows it. The man lectures me constantly about settling down and how I'm asking to be put in the position I've now found myself in. He's going to tell me he told me so.

"I'm going to call them. I just wanted to make sure it was for sure. I thought about keeping it from them, but my mom would be crushed. As it is, Adeline is six months along already."

"Your mom is going to spoil the baby," Miles adds.

I nod, knowing he's right. Between my brother, Ollie, being ten years younger than me and me being the playboy of the league, she's resigned herself to being the best great-aunt she can be to my cousin's kids, but what mother doesn't want to be a grand-mother someday?

"Good luck. He might just take your black card away." Cooper laughs.

I shake my head as Ellery returns with a tray full of shots. My dad won't take my black card away, but what I'm really worried about is how Adeline will feel about the fact that the baby growing in her stomach will have a trust fund with more money in it than she'd make in her lifetime as a teacher solely because his or her last name will be Siska.

Then it occurs to me that we're not married—what if she doesn't want our baby to have my last name? There's so much to figure out, and in some ways, it's even more difficult because we're not in a relationship with each other. But we never will be, so we might as well start sorting it out now.

———

I have the choice to tell my parents face-to-face or in a phone call. I opt for FaceTime as the best of both worlds. They're sheltered in their East Coast mansion, and I'm far away in Chicago.

My gut clenches as my mom's phone rings. It's Sunday, so they should both be home today.

She answers on the second ring. "I was just thinking about how I raised you better. It's been over two weeks with no word from you." She's smiling, her blond hair with sprinkled gray cut in a neat bob and her face fully made up.

"Sorry, I've been busy."

She rolls her eyes. "A mother doesn't want to hear what or who has been keeping you busy."

"I'm not sure about that," I say without thinking of how she could misconstrue that, but her raised eyebrows and small "O" of her lips says she got the wrong idea. "I'm not seeing anyone."

Her shoulders fall. "Oh."

"Boy, I'm just full of disappointments."

She stares at me with that look. The one that says she'll always be proud of me, but they're hopeful to get me out of the trench I've been stuck in for so long.

"Oh, Otis just came in." She turns and looks behind her at the dog. "Otis, it's Damon!"

When Otis reaches her, he sticks his entire face into the camera view and licks the screen.

"Hey, Otis. How is the training going?"

My mom rolls her eyes and pats his head. "We're getting there, right?"

"Sure, you are." I chuckle, not believing a word of it.

She laughs because Otis has failed obedience school twice, and two personal trainers have told Mom there's nothing they can do. Now, she has him with some specialist who has their own show on television. The dog is the most loving thing, but not very well-behaved and always gets into everything.

"Is Dad around?"

My mom's laugh fades, and she stares at me as though she'll be able to see whatever I'm about to tell them. "He's in his office. Why?"

"I need to talk to you both."

With a worried expression, she stands and takes her phone with her as she walks through their mansion, Otis trailing behind her. "This scares me," she says softly, as if I can't hear her. "Is whatever this is the reason why you haven't come home?"

Then I hear my dad screaming when she gets nearer to his office.

"Oh boy," she says. "I think your brother is home."

I arch an eyebrow. "Meaning?"

"Well, he's been at our condo in New York City, and Dad got reports from the neighbors about parties with strippers and stuff." She whispers the word stripper.

That's my brother's MO. He refuses to grow the fuck up and lives off my parents' money. Being ten years younger than me, he's given them way more problems than I ever did. He was thrown out of two boarding schools and just got kicked out of my dad's alma mater. Ollie apparently informed my dad that he will no longer be going to college because he considers it to be a waste.

"Maybe I should call back."

"Nonsense." She knocks on the office door and walks in without waiting for a reply. "I've got Damon on FaceTime."

"It's your golden boy, talk to him. I'll be in my room."

"*Ollie!*" my dad yells.

My little brother's face peeks on the screen. "You look like shit."

"I could say the same."

"See you."

"We are not through here, Oliver! You will pay for all the damage to our condo," my dad screams.

The slam of the door says that Ollie's left.

"I swear, your son," my dad says.

"*My* son?" My mom points at herself.

"I'm taking credit for this one." Mom smiles at the screen.

"And what does your golden boy want?" my dad asks.

My mom laughs and positions the phone on his desk, bringing a chair next to him and taking a seat. "He says he has news."

My dad pinches the bridge of his nose. "Just what I need, more shitty news."

"How do you know it's shitty?" I ask with a frown.

"Because your ass would be in the chair across from me if it was good news. You're in the offseason, Damon, and last time I checked, you had the means to either pay for a public flight or have the private plane come and get you. So, just lay it out there. Your brother's already escalated my migraine." He tips his head down and rubs his temples.

"It's not horrible news, it's just…"

"Spit. It. Out." He stares at me through the screen. My dad still has his dirty-blond hair without any gray, and he's fit from running every morning, but today he looks older than he usually does. When I can't get the words out, he asks, "Do I need a scotch?"

I decide to just go with my usual humor.

"Congratulations, you're going to be a grandpa and grandma!" I put up my hands as though it's exciting news.

"What?" My mom's eyes widen, and she beams. "Oh my god! This is great." Then her smile dims. "You're not talking about a dog or cat or a fish, are you?"

I laugh. "No, Mom. A real, live human being."

Her smile reappears, and it lights up the entire screen, warming my chest.

But my dad just sits there, staring. He scratches his head. "Son, who's the baby's mother?"

I knew my mom would only hear the word baby, but my dad would hear baby mama along with trust fund, rich, user, opportunist.

"She's a woman I met last summer right before the season started." I keep my voice light.

"Are you dating her?" he asks.

"No." I swallow hard.

He frowns. "*Were* you dating her?"

"No." I suck in a big breath.

My mom's smile drops, and I see my dad's hand squeeze my mom's leg. I hate that they're disappointed in me. It's like a crushing feeling in my chest.

"Maybe we should talk privately," my dad says, looking at my mom.

Her head rears back. "Oh no, you don't. I'm not being pushed out into the next room like I can't handle the news that my son knocked up one of his one-night stands. I don't live in a cave, Stanley. I read the articles and hear the rumors."

"Yes, your son can't keep his dick out of every fresh piece of ass he sees."

And there's the look on my phone screen I dreaded—complete and total disappointment.

CHAPTER 8
ADELINE

ONE MONTH LATER

"This wasn't necessary," I say to my mom as she flits around my parents' modest three-bedroom house, making sure everything looks presentable. "I mean, Damon's family is—"

"I know, Adeline. They're wealthy, but I didn't see them planning the shower." She takes out the dips and places them on the table. "Not to mention, you're both trying to keep this from the media, so it's not like I could rent a place."

I grab a carrot and dunk it in my mom's

special dip that I love. "I'm sorry. I'm just nervous."

She sits in the chair next to mine. "That's understandable. This is all very unconventional."

"Please don't say it." I can't bear for her to tell me again how it's nice to get to know a person before having their baby.

"I'm not. But having a baby is stressful. Merging families is stressful. There are a lot of changes coming your way, and I think he has a lot of growing up to do."

"Mom…"

"Give the boy a break, Marge. He's a professional athlete. He didn't get there being lazy," my dad chimes in from his recliner.

"Okay. Okay." She holds her hands up in front of her. "I'm going to leave my opinions to myself. He did impress me at the doctor's appointment. But I would've thought you might bring him around more over the last month." She gives me her mom look.

"We're both busy." I shift in my seat to try to get more comfortable.

She looks down her nose at me. "It's his offseason."

"And need I remind you that we're having a baby together, but we're not a couple? I can't very well tell him to come to Sunday dinner. He hasn't missed a doctor's appointment. He's taken over all the payments my insurance isn't covering. He came with me when I registered for this baby shower." I refrain from mentioning that he had not one clue what we needed and looked disinterested until we reached the toy area.

"Yeah. I just don't know how you're going to make it work."

My shoulders sink. Then the doorbell rings, and I say a small prayer of thanks for the end to this conversation.

"I'll get it." I get off the stool and walk to the front door—waddle is more like it.

I open the door to find Damon standing there alone.

"They're getting out of the car now, but I wanted to apologize ahead of time," he says rapidly.

"What? Why?"

"My dad demanded we come early so we could all have a sit-down. You, your parents, me, and my parents."

I cross my arms. "What are we, like, fifteen?"

"Exactly." He rolls his eyes.

"Damon, I raised you better than this. Why'd you just rush off—oh..." A blonde woman turns the corner of the house onto the pathway and comes into view. She has a long gray wool coat belted around her slim waist, slacks, and heels. Beautiful diamond earrings hang off her ears, and her makeup is subtle but perfectly applied. "Adeline?"

I place my hand over my stomach and my cotton dress that I bought at a store she's probably never been inside in her life. "Hi."

Damon places his arm around my waist, standing at my side. "Mom, this is Adeline. Adeline, this is my mom, Heather."

His mom's smile never falters as I hold out my hand. She shoos it away, wrapping me in a hug. "I'm so happy to meet you." She pulls back and studies me. "You're one of the lucky ones, only holding the weight in your belly." She drops my arms. "Damon had me as big as a house. My legs were swollen, it was horrible."

I didn't realize until I got pregnant how many people feel the need to comment on your body and your weight without being asked.

"Jesus Christ, you two." A man who is the spitting image of Damon but a couple decades older comes around the corner. "We could present as a family." He wears a button-down shirt tucked into his slacks with a belt and a sweater over it, his long coat open. He's an attractive man for his age, which probably means Damon will continue to be blessed with his good looks.

"Come meet Adeline." Heather's eyes never stray from me, but neither does her welcoming smile.

"Adeline." He nods and holds out his hand. "I'm Stanley."

"You can call him Stan," Heather offers, and I'm pretty sure Stanley growls.

We shake hands.

"Nice to meet you," he says, and I hope that's a good sign.

"Please come in." I step back but fumble on a shoe behind me. Damon is there, catching me before I fall over. "Thanks," I say, looking up at him.

"Oh, you must be Marge." Heather

breaks the distance and hugs my mom the same way she did me.

"My mom can be a bit much," Damon whispers.

"She's very nice." I shut the door. "Can I take your coat, Mr. Siska?"

"Sure." He takes his arms out of the coat, but Damon grabs it before I can.

"Mom, coat?" He waits for her.

Heather continues to talk to my mom while taking off her coat. She's wearing a white silk top with taupe slacks that taper at the ankle. Her high heels make her tower over my mom, but she still looks short compared to her son and husband.

"I'm sorry our other son, Oliver, couldn't make it, but he said he was sending a gift," Heather says.

"That my parents probably bought," Damon whispers in my ear. He hasn't told me much about his parents or his brother.

After all the introductions are made, Mr. Siska points at the dining room table. "Can we all sit a moment?"

My mom looks at me, and I shrug. We head over to the table, each family standing on either side of the table. I really do feel as if I'm sixteen and pregnant, and our parents are going to tell us exactly how this is going to go.

"Can I get either of you something to drink?" my mom asks.

"I'll have iced tea, please," Heather says.

"Do you have some scotch?" Stanley asks.

Both Heather and Damon look at his dad.

"Fine, iced tea is good for me too," he says.

"No, I've got some scotch," my dad says, going to the locked cabinet in our kitchen. My parents aren't big drinkers, and if they do, it's usually beer or wine.

Stanley sits at the end of the table as if he's the head of the household. He's intimidating, I'll give him that. From what I read online, the Siskas are old money. Stanley's family was big in the steel business, affording them the life they now live.

My dad finds a bottle of scotch, and I smile to myself as he pours two glasses and sits back down. Damon sits with his mother on one side, and I sit with my mother on the other side.

His dad sips his scotch and sits up straight. "My son and my wife are going to be upset with me for bringing these items up today, but I'm a believer that once you get the business out of the way and everyone is on the same page, it's easier to enjoy yourself. Which is why I wanted to show up before the shower started."

Damon looks at me with an apology in his eyes.

"Adeline, you seem like a fine person, but you're a stranger to us."

"Stanley," Heather says through gritted teeth, still managing a smile.

"I would have demanded a paternity test, but Damon says you've had one and the baby is his. The fact that you're carrying a Siska heir means a few things. First is that a trust fund will be set up as soon as he or she is born. It will be in the child's name only, and the only people who will have access to manage it will be Heather, Damon, and myself."

"Dad…" Again, Damon's eyes find mine.

"My son doesn't like to discuss these things because he's made his own money, but let's be clear, he has a trust fund as well that's been available since he was twenty-five. He's fortunate to have made money doing what he loves, but it also makes him naive to the fact that people would try to slide into our family to get a piece of our pie."

"Stanley!" Heather appears mortified.

"Dad," Damon practically growls.

"Excuse me," my dad says, putting up his hand. "Are you suggesting that my daughter purposely got pregnant by Damon for your family's money?"

Stanley shakes his head. "No, my point is that my son doesn't know the lengths people have gone to over the years. Right now, I am the patriarch of my family, which means I'm in the position of being the protector." He turns to me, and I try to muster up a smile. "Now I think you're a very sweet girl, and upon meeting you and hearing everything Damon had to say about you, I'm thankful it's you who will bear Damon's offspring. God knows the women he's been seen with over the years could've been a hell of a lot worse. Which is why I want to also offer you the benefits of being in the Siska circle."

"Can't this wait until the baby is born?" Damon asks.

I wonder how much of what his father is going to tell me he already knows.

"No harm in getting the idea out there. Adeline, you can leave teaching and raise the baby full-time. I know Heather loved being a stay-at-home mom. Although we had nannies too, and Damon will tell you how much he loved Miss Jillian. Or maybe as he or she gets older, you'll want to consider boarding school like we did with our youngest, Oliver."

Heather slouches in her chair, practically burying her head in her iced tea. Damon's back is straight, and his eyes look murderous as he gazes on at his father.

"You want me to quit my job?" I choke out.

My mom places her hand over mine in a show of support. I'm actually surprised she hasn't been more vocal during this entire exchange.

"No. You do what you want." He shakes his head. "But it won't be easy raising the child with Damon's schedule. We're happy to offer nanny services if you'd rather continue to work."

"I can handle all this, and anyway, it's between Adeline and me," Damon says.

His dad exhales a deep breath, seeming annoyed and exhausted that Damon keeps trying to circumvent this conversation. Have they had this fight before? I wouldn't know because he's told me nothing about his family.

Sure, I knew they had old money. The articles from when he was drafted said he didn't need the million-dollar contracts. Reporters even dug up how much he would be given when he reached twenty-five. When I read it all, I felt bad for Damon that people knew so much about him without really *knowing* him.

"Damon thinks he knows what needs to be done in this situation, but the truth is, if he'd listened to me, he wouldn't be in this situation in the first place." He raises his hand at Damon when he opens his mouth. "That doesn't mean Heather and I aren't happy about the baby, but I think we can all agree that it's not ideal." He sips the scotch. At least he didn't turn his nose up at my dad for his selection of alcohol. "Please, let me know what you think."

I take a moment to order my thoughts before I end up yelling and crying from frustration as I flee the room. Stanley Siska wouldn't respect someone like that, and like it or not, this man is going to be in my child's life.

"First of all, I didn't know about the Siska money when I slept with Damon. Sure, he's a professional football player and well-known enough that I'd seen his jerseys worn by a lot of students in my school, so I knew he had his own money. But I didn't plan on getting pregnant. In fact, he's about the last person a woman would choose to be the father of their baby. Not for any reason except that he's a Peter Pan and not nearly ready to settle down."

His dad nods and looks at his son.

When I see the hurt flash across Damon's face, I wish I hadn't said that. I have to force myself to continue. "But so far, he's been responsible. He hasn't missed one doctor's appointment. He asks me what I need every time he sees me. He's concerned about my health. All of that makes me think I don't know the real Damon Siska. Even now, I see him barely able to contain himself in that chair, respecting you enough not to yell at you for coming into my family's house and holding court as if it's your own. I don't expect anything from your family. Should you choose to give the baby a trust fund and I not have any control of it, so be it. I don't care. But I'm not going to quit my job. I can be a mother and a teacher at the same time. I don't need anything from the Siska family except a loving father and grandparents."

His dad leans back in the chair and finishes off his scotch, then a slow smile forms on his lips before he busts out laughing. "Welcome to the family, Adeline."

CHAPTER 9
DAMON

The guests started arriving before I managed to take Adeline to the side and apologize for my dad. I told him when I picked them up at the airport that he was to enjoy today and get to know Adeline and her family—keep all the legal shit to himself. I guess he didn't get into too much legal stuff, but the whole quit your job and send the baby to boarding school? What the fuck?

Then I remember my father and grandfather yelling in my grandfather's study. They always disagreed, and I distinctly recall my grandfather telling me that one day my dad would understand—when the empire was all his to worry about. I didn't understand it until my grandfather had a heart attack and died, leaving my dad in charge when I was in high school.

Finally, once everyone has arrived and she's made the initial rounds, I'm able to corner Adeline in the kitchen as she's getting someone a drink.

"Adeline," I say, and she turns to me, her cheeks pink from either how hot the room is or the fact she's still embarrassed. I really hope it's the former. "I'm sorry about my dad."

She shakes her head, pouring club soda into a solo cup. The bottle slips from her grasp and falls to the floor, pouring everywhere, including on her dress. "Fuck."

The word shocks me because I don't think I've heard Adeline swear. I take it as a sign as to how much the conversation with my dad has affected her.

"I don't want to talk about it right now. I just want to get through this shower."

"You go and clean up, and I'll get this. Who's the drink for?"

"Isla," she says and moves to walk around me.

"My favorite person," I mumble.

"Now we each have someone on the other side we're not fond of." She walks off, and my anger fumes. It's one thing for me not to like her friend, it's another for her not to like the grandfather of her baby. I've got to get my dad under control.

The worst part about today is that none of my friends could come. I only invited Miles, Bryce, Cooper, and Ellery because they're the only ones who know I've fathered a baby with my one-night stand, but Miles is away with Bryce attending her parents' wedding, Ellery is working, and Cooper has a photoshoot for one of his sponsors. My other teammates would be standing in line to razz me and tell me it's about time I get what I deserve.

My mom is with Isla in the corner of the living room. She finds friends wherever she goes.

"Here's your drink," I say, handing it to Isla.

Her eyebrows draw down. "You didn't spit in it, did you?"

God, I hate this woman.

"Last I checked, I wasn't twelve." I slide

my hands into my pockets and rock back on my heels.

"Sweetie," my mom says, and I roll my eyes because she has no idea how much I dislike this woman.

Isla's had it out for me from the moment I met Adeline. And it's not just her attitude toward me either. I think she's a shit friend to Adeline as well. It's one thing to be protective of your friend and another to reprimand an adult for her decisions.

"That's funny, from everything I've read about you, your intelligence level seems to be about that."

"Okay, so it goes both ways then. Got it." My mom nods.

Adeline comes out from down the hall, and I stop her by her elbow, directing her away to ask her something, anything, to get away from Isla. I go with the first thing that comes to mind.

"Hey, did you ever find out who sent me the text?" I can totally see Isla sending it out of spite or to mess with Adeline.

She shakes her head. "I asked Isla and Sami. I was at a bowling party at the time. I might have put my phone down for a second, but whoever did it was able to figure out my password and knew that I had your number, or at least I guess they assumed I did. Anyway, both of them said no."

"Do you believe them?"

She thinks for a moment. "Why would they lie? Plus, what's the advantage of someone texting you? I never said I was keeping it from you forever. I had plans to reach out that following week anyway."

"Present time!" Adeline's mom calls from the other side of the room.

"Thank God, then cake, and today is over," Adeline says, walking away from me.

I frown. Aren't baby showers supposed to be fun for the mom-to-be?

"Adeline and Damon, both of you sit on the couch," Marge says.

I nod. "Thanks."

The stack of presents isn't huge because not that many people are here. My mom has already told me what she's giving us, and at this point, I worry how it's going to go over thanks to the conversation earlier with my dad.

Marge pulls out a sheet of paper and a pen, which I figure out quickly is to write down who gave what. This whole thing is foreign to me, but Adeline seems to be enjoying herself now. Who doesn't love presents, I guess, right?

There're a lot of clothes, and since we don't know what we're having, the colors are mostly yellow, light greens, and creams. Her parents give us a stroller, which I can't figure out how to fucking open. Needless to say, there's a lot of other stuff I didn't even know we would need, and two of everything since we don't live in the same house. When I stared at the identical boxes of baby monitors, it made my chest ache for some reason.

Marge sets my mom's envelope on Adeline's lap, and I freeze in fear that my family is going to push her out of my life. That it will all be too much for her, and she'll want to seize control. I've been around our family's money my entire life and my parents aren't being overbearing on purpose. They honestly just want to share their wealth with their first grandchild and the woman who's bringing him into the world. But not everyone sees it that way, especially when you don't come from my world. Lots of people associate money with power, and Adeline could think my family is trying to manipulate her with their money.

"This is from Damon's parents, Stanley and Heather."

Adeline smiles at my mom. She opens the envelope and reads what's inside, then looks at her own mother before her gaze shifts to my mom. "Thank you. It's very generous."

Okay, good, she didn't run.

Adeline holds out the letter, which is a gift certificate from an interior designer, and tells the room, "It's to have the baby's room done with all the furniture and painting and everything."

"Well, Damon isn't going to be any help in the painting department, and Stanley and I really wanted to buy the furniture, but we didn't see any on your registry," my mom says. "This felt like the easiest thing. She's expecting your phone call on Monday." My mom sips her iced tea. She's proud of herself, and the gift is very thoughtful, even though she just slammed me.

"I can paint," I say.

The room fills with laughter, stirring my irritation.

"Yeah, but why when you can pay someone to do it for you, right?" Isla says.

I growl under my breath. I hate that woman. And I'm going to show them what I'm capable of when I make up the baby's room at my apartment.

———

I drive Adeline home with all the presents and arrange for an Uber Black to take my parents downtown to their hotel.

Adeline hasn't invited me to her place yet, and I'm eager to see how she lives. I follow her directions to a small two-story house painted white with black shutters and a small detached one-car garage at the end of the driveway. It's in the downtown area of her town, and it's cute and quaint like I'd expect.

"This is it. Home sweet home." She opens the door and gets out of the vehicle.

I'm thankful that with the change of weather, we've had some warmer days, so I no longer have to worry about her slipping on ice.

She unlocks the front door as I work on bringing everything in from the vehicle. As soon as she's inside, she flops onto her couch and slips off the flats she's wearing. "I swear, I hate feeling this unattractive. Even my shoes are ugly now because of my swollen feet."

"Oh please, you're beautiful."

She laughs, and I go out to the car to grab the stroller. The one I'm determined to master in the next month or two.

Adeline sits on the couch, taking out the clothes and pulling off the tags. "Now I kind of wish we would've found out. All this yellow."

I chuckle. "We can get more clothes after he or she is born." I continue to fiddle with the stroller.

"You're going to break that thing," she warns, watching me grow more and more frustrated.

I finally put it aside. "I just don't get it. Why make something so hard to open when you most likely have a baby in your arms when you have to open it?"

Now that I'm not deep in my determination to beat the stroller, I let my gaze roam over the house. Her living area, dining room, and kitchen take up the majority of the wide, open-concept first floor, with a staircase along the wall.

"How many bedrooms are here?"

She glares at me. "Don't start. I'm not moving if that's what you're suggesting. I won't let your family buy me some new house and supply me with maids and butlers."

I sit in the chair adjacent to her, my face falling. "I'm sorry about my parents."

She heaves out a sigh. "Don't be. I know they mean well. They could've come here thinking I manipulated you into sleeping with me to get pregnant."

I chuckle, remembering how she schooled my dad. "That type of woman wouldn't have stood up for herself today. I couldn't have done it better myself."

She huffs. "He's protective, and that's not a bad thing. The biggest problem I see right now, Damon, is that we're two strangers who are about to raise a child together. Most couples suffer through the sleepless nights of a newborn already knowing each other and having a loving relationship to draw on. How will we have patience for one another? Are we even on the same page as to how we want to raise this baby? There are so many questions we need to answer—visitation, insurance, money. I'm starting to get nervous that we don't have a plan." She chews on the inside of her cheek.

I shift over to the couch and grab her legs, forcing them onto my lap so I can massage her feet.

Her head falls back to the pillow, and her eyes close. "Are you trying to distract my Type A brain? If so, it's not going to work. The thoughts will just come back, but feel free to continue." She chuckles.

"I don't have all the answers, and there're definitely things we need to discuss. How about we plan on having two to three nights a week together to get to know one another? We can decide what's best for our baby. We don't need our parents' approval on what's going to work for us. If we want help, which I will need when the baby is with me, we'll hire nannies. But first things first, let's get to know one another a little better before we go into freak-out mode, okay?"

I dig into her arches, and she sighs. "Since you're being so kind as to massage my feet, I'm going to let the whole freak-out mode comment go for now."

I chuckle and run my finger up her arch to see if she's ticklish. She tries to remove her foot from my hand, and I smile because I now know one more thing about her.

"What's your favorite food besides a Reuben?" I ask to start the ball rolling.

We spend the next two hours finding out all the stuff you usually discover on the first few dates. She finally yawns, and I say good night. I'm climbing back into my Mercedes when my phone dings. I pull it out of my pocket to see a text from Bryce.

> It wasn't me. I swear. But it's going live tomorrow morning, and I wanted you to know.

My stomach sinks.

The next text comes through with a few

pictures of Adeline and me together. One is even from outside the school that first day. The caption reads, *Say goodbye, girls, Chicago Grizzlies greatest "player" is going to be a daddy.*

I turn off the ignition and knock on Adeline's door. Guess I'm going to see if Adeline will let me sleep on the couch tonight in case the press come knocking.

CHAPTER 10
ADELINE

It turns out there's something worse than getting knocked up by your one-night stand who happens to be a professional football player—getting outed and having people write horrible, nasty comments about you.

There's nothing quite like being eight months pregnant, feeling as if you weigh as much as an elephant, being swollen from fingers to toes, and having women pick out each and every flaw you've been self-conscious about.

"You need to stop." Damon tries to take my phone for the millionth time, but I snatch it back. "They're just jealous."

"Well, how does it feel to be the prized bull every female cow wants to mate with?"

"Then I guess you should feel good because I impregnated you, not them."

I glare at him from the corner of my eye.

He laughs. "I'm kidding. Don't listen to these women. I've seen girlfriends and wives of teammates go through this a zillion times. You have to ignore it. You cannot let their perception become your reality. Bryce went through it with Miles."

"Bryce wasn't as big as a house. I mean, what are the chances they shoot me at my worst angle every shot?" I whine. I hold up my phone with the picture of me outside Ira's. People have commented how big the bag is and how someone there said I ordered three sandwiches for myself.

"You're going to make me call the cell phone company and shut down your service."

"God, Damon." I turn off my screen. "I didn't really think it would be like this. I mean, I knew it would garner attention, and I figured some people would say I got pregnant on purpose, but these people are just brutal."

He takes the opportunity to steal my phone, but we both know he'll have to give it back at some point. "It will blow over, and they'll be on to someone else."

"I guess."

The doorbell rings, and I jolt up.

Damon's hand lands on my knee. "Relax, it's just the groceries I ordered."

My forehead wrinkles. "What?"

"I figured you wouldn't want to go out." He opens my door, and he tips the guy standing there.

His eyes slowly widen when he notices who handed him the money. "Damon Siska?"

The delivery guy pats his pockets. With a lot of effort, I stand and grab a notepad and a pen from the table near my door and hand them to Damon.

"I'm only going to sign this if you don't tell anyone I'm here," Damon says to the guy who incessantly nods. Damon scribbles his signature and number on the piece of paper and hands it over.

The man thanks him and walks down the steps.

I step out to grab some of the bags of groceries when I hear the flutter of a camera lens. I glance to my left and see it's my elderly neighbor. "Mrs. Turnberry?"

"Sorry, darling, but my bridge club didn't believe me when I messaged them last night that Damon Siska just walked into my neighbor's house."

"Do they have a problem with how big I am too? How about my nose? Or my lips? Or my hair? Is my forehead too small or too big? There's a poll going on right now. Maybe they'd like to cast a vote."

She brings her camera down with a frown. "You're gorgeous, and they think so too. They're just avid football fans."

I huff out a sigh. "I'm sorry. I'm just on edge."

Damon steps out and smiles at my elderly neighbor. "Are people bothering you?" he asks her.

Her mouth falls open. I guess there are times I forget how well-known he is. "Do you play bridge?"

He takes a quick, confused glance at me before he answers. "I'm sorry, I don't. Rummy?"

"That's for amateurs." Mrs. Turnberry

waves him off. "Well, I have to go show these off to my friends, especially Pearl. She flat-out told everyone I was lying, questioning why Damon Siska was in our small town." She winks. "Because of our stunning Adeline Morgan, that's why."

I can't fight my smile. After being pummeled like that mole game at arcades, my self-confidence has taken a beating. "Thanks. Mrs. Turnberry."

Then she gets a fierce expression. "And I'll take care of anyone if they come snooping around. I have no problem being the crazy old neighbor with a broomstick." She smiles one last time and walks back into her house.

"Interesting neighbor," Damon says, waiting for me to go inside first.

We put away the groceries together, him mostly unpacking since he doesn't know where anything goes and me placing them in the cupboards. When I come across a lot of what must be ingredients for a dish, I pick up two bulbs of garlic and turn to him. "What are these for?"

"I'm going to make you dinner tonight."

He smiles, and it gives me this fluttery feeling in my chest.

"Damon." I shake my head. "You don't have to babysit me. I'm not going to harm myself over some virtual bullies."

He hands me the yogurt I eat every morning. Someone was snooping. "I want to. I just want to make sure no one bothers you and the baby." His eyes are imploring me to let him do this for me.

"Okay."

He's being a gentleman, but I'm sure it's out of guilt. I'm not the first woman to get knocked up by a professional athlete. I doubt I'll wake up to the paparazzi outside my house.

———

We spend the day watching television and playing rummy, then Damon insists I take a long bath while he makes dinner.

When I'm finished, I call down from the top of the stairs, still in my robe, "It going okay down there?"

"Perfect. I've done this a thousand times.

Wear something comfy. Siska Bistro isn't strict on dress code."

I smile and head to my room, where I lotion my belly and the rest of my body to hopefully keep stretch marks at bay. I've already noticed a few on my stomach as it gets bigger. I put on a pair of leggings and a T-shirt that reads, "I'll be a lot more fun when I can drink again."

Just as I head downstairs, the doorbell rings. Damon rushes out of the kitchen with a dish towel over his shoulder, looking every bit the part of a domesticated man. It makes my insides purr.

"I'll get it," I say, closer to the front of the house.

I open the door, and there's a man with two suitcases. "Evening, I'm looking for Damon Siska?"

"Thanks, Nick." Damon comes up behind me. His hand lands on the small of my back as he slides by me, putting his hands out for the suitcases.

"No problem. If you need anything else, just let me know. But I'm leaving tomorrow with your parents."

Damon nods, sliding the suitcases into the house. "I'm good. Sorry to bother you."

"It's a good thing you sent me. Peeper's Alley was packed when I went by your place."

"Why? What are the suitcases for?" I ask, unclear as to what's going on and who Nick is.

"Sorry, Nick, this is Adeline. Adeline, this is my parents' personal assistant, Nick."

I shake his hand. "Nice to meet you."

"Pleasure's mine. Congratulations," he says with a smile. Then he nods to Damon to step outside with him.

Damon walks outside and shuts the door behind him. I look around as if I'm missing something. What has happened to the control I had over my life? I stare at the suitcases. Those can only mean one of two things: Damon has to go on a trip and he's leaving right from here, or he's moving in. I really hope it's the former.

I'm in the kitchen stirring the red sauce when the front door shuts.

"Hey now, don't mess with perfection." Damon gently knocks his hip against mine to move me away from the stove.

"What's going on?"

"We'll talk while we eat. It's time to plate. If you take the salad, I'll prepare our pasta plates." He hands me a bowl of salad that isn't a bag mix, but one he's made himself.

"You're just full of surprises." I sit at my small table that can fit four but really only two comfortably. It's then I notice that all the blinds are shut.

"What do you mean?" He glances over his shoulder while spooning the sauce onto the noodles.

"I assumed you'd be the kind of person who got catering from a restaurant and pawned it off as his own cooking. I mean…" I stop myself from saying more. Damon Siska is not at all the man I thought he was. I don't know what to do with that yet.

"What else did you think about me?"

I sigh. "Honestly?"

He places a steaming plate of spaghetti in front of me. "Yes, my ego can take the hit."

"I thought I was going to tell you I was pregnant, and you'd disappear. I figured you'd pay child support after the paternity test, and maybe you'd try to see the baby a few times, but eventually, you'd go on with your life and we'd go on with ours."

I feel bad after the words leave my mouth, but I think it's best to be honest. I never would have thought he'd stay here after the news broke to make sure I was okay. He's being protective, and it's making me like him. Too much.

"Well, I'm glad I'm surprising you." He smiles and nods toward the dish, not seeming to be affected by my words. "Now eat. Pretty soon, I'm going to count your calories for you."

"Believe me, I eat."

He shakes his head. "Not today, you haven't."

I hadn't realized he'd be so observant either.

We each dig in, and it's so good that I can't hide my moan. "Mmm, Damon, this is amazing."

"Keep making those noises, and I'm not going to be able to be a gentleman."

I laugh. "Sorry."

"Don't be. It just takes me back to that night."

Our gazes lock and hold.

"I can't be the only one who makes all those noises in bed with you." Best to remind my libido that I'm nothing special. I stab my fork in the salad and bring it to my lips. The tangy homemade dressing over the crisp lettuce is to die for.

"You were different. I knew it as soon as you left."

I feel my cheeks heat. I need to change the subject before this goes too far. I'm so horny lately, and my nipples are so sensitive. It would take nothing for him to get me off at this point, and that kind of thinking can only lead to trouble—and confusion.

"So, Nick?" I try to change the subject.

He clearly knows what I'm doing because he laughs before leaning back and sipping his water. I wonder if he's not drinking because I can't, or if he just doesn't drink as much as I assumed he did. "I needed my things, and I knew the bar downstairs would be crowded with people trying to take a picture of me or us together. I called in a favor."

"What was it like growing up like that?"

He stares at his plate for a second,

moving his pasta around. "I can't complain. To have what you want all the time isn't a bad way of life. I was privileged, to be sure. When my grandfather died at the same time colleges started paying attention to my football skills, it worked in my favor. I'd been my dad's entire focus up until that point—sending me to camps and lining me up with professional instructors. After my grandfather died, my dad had to take the reins of the family, so he didn't have a lot of time for me. I think that benefited me a lot."

"Why? Sounds like he was trying to give you every advantage." I fork some more pasta into my mouth and suppress the urge to moan at the taste.

He nods, and his gaze meets mine. "Yeah, but your teammates don't respect the kids who get on teams because of their parents. No one likes the coach's kid who gets to play a position because his dad is the coach, especially when they suck at it. Him being distracted allowed me to follow the same path as everyone else. I got into Michigan because they sought me out, not the other way around. I feel like I made it myself, you know. I didn't get there on Daddy's money."

"Money doesn't make someone talented."

He chuckles. "I suppose not, but it can buy off a lot of people. If I was a shit player, I wouldn't have made it to the pros, or if I did, I would've ridden the bench. It's the one thing I can really pride myself on because to get where I did is hard as hell. That's why I couldn't give two shits what people say about my game."

"Like the fans?"

"Yeah, I mean, it's like all that shit those women are saying about you. We have to deal with the Monday morning quarterbacks who talk shit with their friends and comment on social media threads as if they could do it better. They didn't have what it takes, or they'd be where I am, so I don't really give a shit what they say."

I think about it for a moment, and his words ring true. Those women just wish they were sitting across from Damon right now. That they were the ones carrying his baby.

"I don't want to hide out," I say, feeling some of my confidence return.

A slow smile spreads on his face, and it makes me wish he was mine to kiss because it's so damn sexy. "You don't have to."

I raise my chin a bit. "I don't care what they say about me. I know myself and…" I run my hands over my belly. "They just want what I have. Let them be jealous."

He slowly claps his hands. "That's my girl."

God, those words and his smile, like he's proud of me make me, want to melt into a puddle. He puts his large hand over my smaller one, and I ignore the way I seem to light up at the small show of affection.

"Damon?" I just have one last question for him regarding today's events.

"Yeah?"

"What are the suitcases for?"

His smile grows wicked. It's the same one he gave me during our night together after he gave me my first orgasm with his mouth between my legs. "I want to move in."

My fork slips from my hand and falls to the plate.

CHAPTER 11
DAMON

've been staying at Adeline's for two weeks, and the due date keeps creeping closer. I hired a trainer out here, and other than once a week when Cooper makes me go into the city to train with him on plays and passes, I'm here. The media attention has died down somewhat, although every time a picture is snapped of us, there are more nasty comments made about Adeline. I wish I could shield her from all this bullshit.

"You have to stop driving me to work," Adeline says as I pull up along the curb of the school. She had a doctor's appointment this morning, and I was filled with relief when the doctor said everything was going well.

"Nope, not gonna happen," I say.

She undoes her seat belt and turns a little in her seat to face me. "Damon, you can go home now."

I shake my head. "I figure I might as well wait it out until the baby arrives."

She sighs. "Why would that be?"

"Are you trying to kick me out? Am I that much of a nuisance?"

"No, but you have your own life. And I feel like you've been neglecting your friends and stuff."

What started out as me wanting to protect her turned into me moving in to do just that, but once I got there, I realized that I've already missed so much of this pregnancy, and I don't want to miss any more. I never would've guessed that domestic life was kinda cool. Maybe it's Adeline who makes it that way.

Every night she has me watching some dramatic reality TV show where we make predictions about how things will go. I either make dinner or we order in. I don't have a lot of cooking skills—I sort of used up my best the first night I cooked for her. But as much as I'm not Bobby Flay, she isn't Julia Child.

"I'm not neglecting anything." Honestly, Miles and Bryce are probably all over one another since they got engaged on their trip away for her parents' wedding, and Cooper spends every available minute with Ellery. If I were being my usual self, I'd be going out to clubs and bars or sporting events, probably getting myself into trouble. "As long as I get my workouts in, I'm good."

She nods. "Okay, then, I have a job for you."

"Anything." I don't know why, but I love it when she asks me to do something for her.

"Paint the baby's room." I open my mouth, but she continues before I get a chance to remind her that my mom paid an interior decorator to take care of everything. "I want us to do it. Or me, but I already know you're not going to let me get up on a ladder to paint. Besides, I'm trying to work all the way up to delivery. That way I can use my family leave now and a little after summer."

I nod. "Okay then, what color do you want?"

"I'm thinking a buttery yellow."

I chuckle. "And you want me to pick out this buttery yellow?" The fuck if I know what makes a yellow buttery.

"I'm not really a picky person. I trust you." She smiles all sweetly. Yeah, there's a lot she's not particular about, but she only eats a certain type of bread at home, and her yogurt and granola are the same brands, so there are some things she's particular about.

"You better tell Shaylene that I'll be coming into the school with samples later today, and she better let me in."

"If you're really worried, just do a few paint samples on the wall and we can decide tonight." She opens her door and gets out. A kid passing by says hello to her, and she waves. "Hi, Micah." Then she looks back into the vehicle. "I forgot, I have to oversee the basketball game tonight. So, I won't be ready to leave until six thirty or so."

"Basketball sounds fun."

She scrunches her forehead. "I mean, it is the championship. Us against our rivals."

"I'll be here. If you don't mind, that is?" I

hate to admit it, but a little live sports action sounds nice even if it's middle schoolers. We rarely go out in public because I hate seeing her read those damn comments afterward, even if she says she's over them.

"Not at all. I'm sure the girls will love it." She smiles.

"Girls?"

She chuckles and shakes her head. "Assumed it was boys' basketball, did you, Siska?" She's never been this playful with me, referring to me by my last name, and I find I really like it. "Because something tells me if this little bean is a girl, you're gonna have her running drills in whatever sport she loves."

I grin. "Damn right."

"Have fun doing whatever you're doing today. See you around four or so?"

"I'll be here."

She shuts the door, and I watch her approach the building. She stops just shy of the door, turning, and I see that damn Henry walking up behind her to talk to her. They head into the building together, and I groan.

That's my baby in her belly, asshole.

———

My phone rings on the way to the gym in the neighboring town. It was the only place that allowed me to pretty much have it to myself with a trainer I felt was worthy of his title. Truth is, the guy should be in the city making a shit-ton of money training a higher caliber of athlete than he does out here.

"What?" I answer, and Miles laughs.

"Just making sure you're still alive," he says.

"Are you lost in a corn maze out there?" Cooper chimes in.

So they're together. Great.

"It's not corn season, dipshit, and yes, I'm alive." I turn down the main street, now able to make my way through town without GPS. "You guys heading to work out?"

"Yeah, you know where *your* ass should be," Cooper says. "You better be here in two days. We're not going to win the bowl again this coming season if you're not training."

"Don't worry about me. You throw the ball, I'll catch it."

Cooper groans. Usually I'm all his during the offseason to practice whatever he wants. We probably won last season because we put in so much effort during the offseason.

"How's the pregnancy?" Miles asks.

"Jesus, you're such a woman," Cooper tells Miles.

"Great, how's engaged life?" I ask him.

"I'm done hearing about all this baby shit. And now Miles is talking about wedding shit. What happened to my single friends?" Cooper asks.

"What the fuck happened with Ellery?" I ask, knowing this has to be the reason for his sour mood.

"She went on a date last weekend," Miles says as I make a right.

"And I don't give a shit. That's not why I'm pissy. I'm mad because the two of you need to get your heads out of your asses. I refuse to be a one-time winner. I'm chasing dreams here." Cooper sounds passionate.

I'm sure some of what he just preached is true, but Ellery going on a date has something to do with his mood, I know it does.

"I'm chasing my dream too," Miles says.

"I'm talking about filling my hand with

championship rings, not an engagement ring."

"I told you I'll be there, and I will," I say. "I won't miss it unless she goes into labor. Okay?"

"So, should we rent out your apartment?" Cooper asks.

"No, I'll be back before the season starts."

"I thought Cavanaugh was whipped, but I think you're worse." Cooper continues on with his sour attitude that I'm not really in the mood for. "I mean, I always thought I'd have you, Siska. A perpetual bachelor."

"First of all, I'm still a bachelor. Second of all, Adeline's having my baby, and the press keeps posting updates like I'm some celebrity, and the women are being brutal in the comments. I'm taking care of my own."

"And I couldn't be prouder of you," Miles says.

I roll my eyes even though he can't see me. "Go to hell."

They both laugh.

"Well, we were just making sure aliens didn't abduct you." Cooper laughs at his own joke. "Maybe one day we can actually meet her. More than just the brief introduction we had the day you guys hooked up."

"Maybe if you're lucky."

"You're being so protective," Miles says. "We're your friends."

"I just have to handle this." I should tell them the truth at this point. "Honestly, I'm not sure what it is, but I feel as though this is where I should be. I get that I got here by fucking up, but I want to be a part of my kid's life, and to do that, I need to know his or her mom. I want us to co-parent well together."

"Damn, I got a tear," Cooper says, and I wish he was in front of me so I could flip him off. "I'm kidding though. It's hard when parents don't get along, when they use the kid against the other one. Keep doing what you're doing, but you better make it to my workouts. Otherwise, I'm gonna surprise you in that town and make a spectacle of myself."

I chuckle and shake my head as I pull into the gym parking lot. "Deal. Thanks, guys."

We say our goodbyes, and I enter the gym where my trainer, Ryan, is tapping his watch. He's an intimidating man, even for me.

"Sorry, Cavanaugh and Rice called me."

He doesn't bother acknowledging my excuse for being late. "Start with the sled pushes as a warm-up," he says and walks away with his protein shake to sit in the chair and watch me.

I'm there for three hours, then head back to Adeline's to shower. I go over to the paint store after that. With the help of the guy who works there, I grab three buttery yellows. Back at her house, I put paint samples on the wall of her second bedroom.

Where is she going to put everything in here? I look over the small space that will fit a baby, but what about when the child gets older? I try to be optimistic—she's told me how much she loves this house and that she and her dad did most of the renovations— but there's no room for her to grow here.

I remind myself it's none of my business. We're not a couple, and the decision isn't mine. I know Adeline will be an excellent mother, and she doesn't need all the space I had growing up in order to do that.

While I have the time, I decide to try my

hand at the stroller again and the pack-n-play, each one having caused me grief over the past few weeks. They make the damn things so complicated.

I arrive at the middle school at four o'clock and walk into the gym. The girls are warming up, and I scan the area. Adeline is huddled with some teachers in one corner of the gym. She gives me the one-minute finger, and I find a seat high in the bleachers so no one can sneak a picture of me without me seeing them.

That douche Henry is at her side, smiling as he tells her something. Her head falls back in laughter, and my chest gets tight. I want to head over there and tell him to take his hand off her forearm, that I'm the one who makes her laugh. That I'll be taking her home tonight.

Shit, what is wrong with me? Unfortunately, I can pinpoint the last time I felt something like this. It's been years, probably since Greta, but I can't deny it—I'm fucking jealous.

No wonder I've avoided caring about someone for so long. This feeling sucks balls.

CHAPTER 12
ADELINE

"This baby is never coming out, I swear." I'm in the teachers' lounge, staring at my enormous belly.

"You'll just have to sleep with him," Sami says. "Doctors say it's a method to spur on labor."

"I'm not sleeping with him." I look around, thankful we're the only ones in here so far.

"Come on, he's been living with you for weeks. Have you had one of those 'just out of the shower' moments where you watch the water drip down his body and all you can think of is how you want to lick it off of him?"

"Jeez, Sami, go get laid," Isla says.

Sami ignores Isla's biting comment. "No close calls? Almost kisses or intimate touches? A little tango in the doorway?"

I laugh at Sami. She's a lover of romance, like me. "He moved in to be nice because of the press. But as attractive as he is, I don't want a guy to love me because I'm having his baby by accident."

Isla rolls her eyes. "She still believes in fairy tales."

"And what's wrong with that?" I frown across the table at her.

"Nothing." Sami pats my arm. "Nothing at all. You wait for that fairy tale, but in the meantime, screw your baby daddy to start labor. There's no harm, and you can't get pregnant again. Win-win." She sips her iced coffee, grinning at me.

"Ugh." I lower my chin to my chest. "My forehead can't even fall to the table because of my belly, and you want me to sleep with him," I whine. "I'd prefer he remember sleeping with the thin version of me, not the one with a swollen belly and stretch marks."

"Definitely not a good plan. Have you

ever thought about sleeping with Henry? He's into you."

I stare open-mouthed at Isla, then Sami. "She's kidding, right?"

"He'd be gentle and sweet, and he's always liked you. I bet he'd even take care of you after the baby's born, and boy wonder takes off to chase pussy."

"Isla!" Sami yelps. "He's done nothing for you to judge him like that."

Isla rolls her eyes. "Can I remind you that you never slept with the real Damon Siska? You slept with someone who pretended to be him." She shakes her head, leaning back in her chair, drinking her coffee. "You protect him like you have a connection to him."

"I'm not protecting him because I feel like I slept with him. Jeez, Isla, you're a real joy-killer. I'm protecting him because he's here. He's living with Adeline, painting the baby's room, making dinners, driving her to and from work. He's doing everything a boyfriend would do."

"Except fucking her." Isla arches an eyebrow.

I pretend her comment doesn't sting, even though it's true. "That would just complicate everything. I'm not a hornball, guys. I can go without sex."

I wish I felt as strongly about that as I did when Damon first reappeared in my life. It's been so hard lately not to let my mind wander back to that night and how good it was between us. Sometimes late at night, especially when he rubs my feet, I want to broach the subject. Or the other night, when he massaged my shoulders and his long fingers slid down the front of me, teasing the edge of my bra, it was all I could do not to adjust myself so that he'd "accidentally" touch my breast.

The teachers' lounge starts filling up, so I struggle up out of my chair to head back to my classroom. I don't particularly feel like being social right now but I have no choice for the rest of the day. We're heading over to the high school with our classes to see where they'll be going to school next year.

"I'll catch you guys later," I say, walking out of the teachers' lounge toward my classroom.

I've always enjoyed the fact Sami and

Isla are opposites. Sami is similar to me and loves everything to do with romance, while Isla is jaded when it comes to love. It made for interesting conversations and allowed me to always see both sides of an issue. But right now, I need the advice of a person who has been in this position. I always thought I'd marry some guy who swept me off my feet, but instead, I got knocked up by a professional football player during a one-night stand.

When the time comes, I head out to the front of the school where the buses are waiting. Shortly after, the eighth grade classes file out of the school and onto the buses.

"Hi, Miss Morgan," Lucy says as she steps onto the bus stairs. "I can't wait to go to the high school. So many cute boys." Her eyes flutter, and she goes to her seat.

"Boy crazy," Henry whispers, coming in behind her.

"We were all run by our hormones at that age though, weren't we?" I say, sliding into the seat next to him. Sami and Isla are on the other bus.

"I think some of us still are." He eyes my stomach, and I tilt my head, barely holding back my scowl. "You're telling me you were thinking with your head when that little miracle was conceived?"

This is the first time he's directly mentioned my decision to sleep with Damon last August. He's always taken the pitying approach to my pregnancy, saying how sorry he felt that I'm in this situation and offering to help me with anything I might need.

"It was definitely hormones, but it's turning out okay." I wrap my arms around my stomach as if I'm shielding my baby from hearing that her daddy probably didn't even know her mommy's last name the night they got together.

"Yeah, I saw him at the girls' basketball championship. He always looks at me like he wants to rip my arms off and feed them to me." He chuckles as if he couldn't care less.

That's a tad dramatic.

"I'm sure that's not it."

"Believe me, the guy doesn't like me. And I know that because once you're at his side, he gets a smug look on his face like he's won."

There's absolutely no way I've been

missing all of this, but I'm not in the mood to argue about it, so I decide not to engage.

"Like once you went over to him that night and you were all giddy with laughter, he'd pin me with an amused stare."

"We're not a couple. We're just trying to figure out this co-parenting thing."

The bus finally starts, which I'm thankful for because I'm getting annoyed. Late pregnancy has apparently made me hornier and more temperamental than usual.

"I'm not blind. He's worked his magic on you. If you think he's changed, I'm here to tell you, as a man, men like that don't change. Sure, maybe now, maybe even for a bit after the baby is born, but he'll get restless, and he'll be done with having his wings clipped. He'll want to spread them wide again and fly to where and who he wants."

Well, thank you for your opinion, Henry. Firmly, I say, "We're not a couple and don't intend to be. As long as he's a good father, that's all I care about."

Lies, all lies, but Henry doesn't need to know that. I already found myself thinking about the what-ifs the other day before I forced myself to get a grip. What the heck was I thinking? Damon Siska is not the guy you double down on.

I don't engage Henry in conversation for the rest of the short trip to the high school.

As the kids file out of the bus, he stops me before we enter the building. "I didn't mean to upset you. It's just… it's frustrating when guys like that give girls like you the wrong idea. It's unfair to everyone involved."

I yank my wrist from his hand. "Thank you, Henry, but you really don't understand our relationship, so I'd appreciate you keeping your opinions to yourself."

I hurry after my class, and we file into the auditorium so the principal can talk to us before we head off on our tour of campus.

———

The kids are behaving, and the tours are going well. Thankfully, we separated from Henry's class once we were finished listening to the principal. If I'm lucky, I'll get my class on another bus and not have to share with him again. The audacity of that man.

"Here's our field house." The senior leading the tour stops just inside the big track area with four basketball courts in between.

"Miss Morgan, it's Damon Siska," Lucy exclaims, raising her hand. "Damon!"

I turn in the direction she's yelling, and sure enough, there's Damon in a pair of dark shorts and a sweat-soaked shirt with no sleeves. He's running sprints with who I'm guessing is the trainer he hired. He mentioned something about his trainer having found a place to work outside today, but I was in a rush getting out of the vehicle this morning, so I wasn't really listening.

"Oh man." Sami comes over to my side. "Just so you know, every teacher here is thinking about him naked and driving into them. Even the guys."

I lightly push her shoulder.

"Seriously, look at him." Her eyes are wide.

The trainer blows the whistle and must notice us and tells Damon. He pulls out his earbuds, glances over, and his eyes find mine.

"See him look at Miss Morgan? I told

you. They're in love," one girl says behind me.

Damon says something to the trainer and jogs over, his attention on me the entire time. "Hey." Then he looks at the group of kids. "Hey, guys. Doing a tour, huh?"

All the girls make a sound I can't quite decipher but it sounds a lot like swooning, and the boys all nod.

"How about I jump on your back and see if you can run that sprint for extra conditioning?" Sami says.

I shake my head at her. "You remember Sami from the baby shower?"

There's a hint of amusement in his eyes. He's probably remembering that she's the one who thought she'd slept with him only to find out it was someone pretending to be him.

"Yeah, hey," he says, putting his hand out but then retracting it. "Sorry, I'm a sweaty mess."

"We can see that," Sami says with almost a purr in her voice.

"Introduce us, Miss Morgan!" someone shouts, and I feel my cheeks heat.

"Hi, kids, I'm Damon Siska." He takes it upon himself, giving me a reprieve.

"My mom says you knocked up Miss Morgan," one kid says.

My eyes widen. "Okay, should we continue the tour?" I say to the senior whose vision is zeroed in on Damon's ass at the moment. Great.

"My dad said it's called a one-night stand."

"My grandma said she's jealous of Miss Morgan to have a hunk like him in bed."

I plead with a higher power to get these kids to stop.

"Are you going to marry her, Damon?"

"If so, are we invited to the wedding?"

"Oh jeez." I become flustered, my face feeling as though it's on fire now. "The tour is continuing over in the field house. Let's let Mr. Siska get back to his training session. We all want the Grizzlies to win, don't we?"

"I'm a Green Bay fan actually," a boy says.

"They suck. Go Grizzlies." A boy approaches Damon with his fist in the air to bump.

Of course, Damon fist bumps him.

"See you later, everyone say goodbye to Mr. Siska," I announce loudly enough that I hope they all hear my teacher voice.

"Bye, Mr. Siska."

I wave to him, and he smiles, looking as if he's trying to keep from laughing, before waving and running back to his trainer.

On the way over to the field house, I caught a few comments from some of the students.

"My aunt said he's going to break her heart," one girl says.

"Yeah, my mom said he's not the type who changes his spots," another girl adds.

Isla comes over to my side. "Well, that was a shitshow."

Sometimes I just cannot handle her, and now is one of those times.

"I think it's like a movie. Who doesn't dream of marrying a professional athlete, especially one as hot as Damon Siska? I want to be Miss Morgan when I grow up," a girl says at the back of the pack with a group of friends who all nod in agreement. "I'm going to follow him on social media."

"Great, now you're giving these girls demented dreams." Isla approaches the girl, lecturing her about making a life for herself and not relying on a guy for happiness.

Somehow, I refrain from punching Isla in the nose. I'm not sure if I'd rather ride back with Henry or Isla. They're both on my shit list now. Maybe I'll be lucky and be with Sami.

CHAPTER 13
DAMON

get out of the shower and dry myself before wrapping the towel around my waist. I have about twenty minutes before I need to pick up Adeline from school. Damn, I forgot how much kids speak their minds. I don't know how she handles teaching them every day.

I open the bathroom door, and a cloud of steam billows out into the hall.

"Oh," Adeline says, stopping in her tracks on her way to her bedroom.

"I was just about to go get you," I say.

"I begged off a little early and took an Uber home. I just needed to get out of there. I texted you, but you must not have seen it if you were in the shower." Her eyes dip down to my chest, and her tongue slides out of her mouth, licking her bottom lip.

God, I want that tongue on me so badly, but I can't let her know that, so I wait for her eyes to come back up to mine, and I smirk, trying to play it off.

She covers her eyes with her hands. "Oh my god." She rushes to her bedroom and slams the door.

I laugh and knock on her door.

"Go away. Go get dressed. Just put some clothes on. I'm so sorry."

"Open the door, Adeline," I say, laughing.

"No. There is nothing funny about this. Stop laughing."

"Make sure you're decent because I'm coming in. Three, two…" I slowly open the door and step into the room.

She's laying on her side, head turned into one of her pillows. Her room is all girly —pink, white, and accents of gold. It's delicate, just like she is.

"Look at me," I say, sitting on the edge of her bed.

"Are you dressed?" she mumbles into the pillow.

"I have a towel on."

She shakes her head. "I can't be trusted. Go get clothes, and we can forget this happened and go back to normal. Maybe go out and get pizza."

I grab the edge of the pillow and take it out from under her. "Stop it. It's a natural reaction. I'm hot. If it was who was wrapped in a towel, the roles would be reversed."

She turns her head away from the bed and stares at me blankly.

"What?"

"First of all, I'd need about three beach towels to wrap around me, and there would be nothing sexy about me."

Jesus, I hate hearing her say these things about herself. She's gorgeous, whether she's pregnant or not.

"Hey." I slide closer and put my finger under her chin, so she looks up at me. She sees my bare chest and inhales a deep breath. "You're beautiful, stunningly gorgeous, especially while you're pregnant. You have this glow about you, and I've laid awake more than one night wondering if that flush covers your entire body. I can't tell you how sexy it is that you're growing our baby in your belly. I mean it, I can't even describe the feeling. To me, you're a knockout."

"You have to say this because I'm carrying your baby," she grumbles.

I chuckle. Maybe I shouldn't, but I figure maybe it's time to tell her the full extent of my thoughts about her. I've been keeping them to myself because I didn't want to make her uncomfortable. "No, I don't. I'm being truthful. When you were in those wrap dresses, I always imagined what would happen if I pulled the tie… would it expose you to me? I can't tell you how many times I've beat off to the image of you riding me with that belly between us. Or wondered how sensitive your tits are and how much I'd enjoy figuring it out. Believe me, living in this house with you can be excruciating."

"But if you're horny, you can just go out and find some woman to sleep with. I can't do that. I'm so ready for this baby to come out so I can be a woman again, not just an incubator."

"First, I'm not going to go and have sex with anyone else. He or she is coming soon."

She stares at her stomach. "I don't think they're ever coming out. I made it too nice in there."

I laugh, and she throws a pillow at me. I catch it, of course, and she pretends to be mad.

"Tell me what started all this. I don't think it's just about you checking me out when I came out of the shower."

"I'm not telling you," she says.

I frown. I knew something was going on. Was it all the stuff the kids were saying earlier today?

"Come on. It'll make this better, then we'll go get that pizza you want." I slide closer to her and take her hand, careful not to let the towel open too much.

She huffs. "I was talking to Sami and Isla about wanting the baby out, saying how I'm sick of being pregnant, and Sami brought up how sex can spur labor on."

"That's not a cliché? It's in every movie or show. I figured it was just bullshit."

"No, it's real, but there're other methods like walking and eating spicy foods."

"Why does sex work?" I ask.

"Supposedly, an orgasm can initiate uterine contractions, and there's some hormone in semen that can soften the cervix. Anyway, Sami is just looking for any reason to get us to have sex. And then we went to the field house, and you were well…"

"Sweaty and gross and probably smelled," I say with a laugh.

She gives me a look as if I'm clueless. "Come on, Damon. You were working out, sweaty, with your clothes clinging to every muscle in your body. I had to keep a hundred teenage girls from pouncing on you. And now I have to look at you in that towel. It's just hard, okay? I haven't had sex since we were together."

Shit, I never thought about that. I didn't know about the baby for six months, so I slept with a few girls. Not as many as she probably thinks, but I never felt the urge to be with someone and been unable to act on it.

"Well, thanks for not sleeping with anyone else while my baby is inside you," I say, and she throws another pillow.

This one I don't catch. It hits my head and drops to the floor.

"You're welcome for my sacrifice." She rolls her eyes.

"So, what you're saying is that you're horny?" I arch an eyebrow.

"Seriously, that's all you got out of this?"

"Kind of, yeah."

She shakes her head at me.

"I know that even after the baby is born, you'll have six weeks or longer before you get cleared for any… activity."

"You sure have done your research," she says.

I did it because I've wanted to cross that line more than once since I've been living with her. There have been many times when I wondered what she'd do if I took her in my arms and kissed her.

I feel my dick stir under the towel. "What if we…" I take her chin in my finger and thumb, locking eyes with her.

"No, Damon." But she doesn't sound so sure.

"I want to give you what you need, and I'll be honest, it's not like the thought hasn't crossed my mind too. Nothing has to change. It's just sex, to please you, make you comfortable, and maybe get our baby out of you." I press my lips to hers, but when my tongue slides out to lick the seam of her lips, she draws back.

I hate how crushing the disappointment feels.

"We want to make this co-parenting thing work. We can't get involved."

I put my hand on her cheek, running my thumb there, and I place my other hand on her stomach. "After our baby is born, we're going to be zombies from lack of sleep. We're going to cater to the baby's needs, and the last thing we're going to think about is sex. So, let's give Mommy an orgasm."

"Don't ever say that combination of words again."

I chuckle, inching forward to kiss her again. "I was just trying it out. Call me Daddy, and let's see if it works the other way around."

"Oh, Daddy, touch me," she says in an overly enthusiastic voice.

"Yeah, okay, we're not into that kink. See? We learned something new about one another. Progress." I place my lips on hers.

She finally opens her mouth, our tongues tangling together, and the relief that jolts through my body, the rightness of the feeling should scare me, but then my libido takes over, wanting to do all the things I've been imagining for months.

I slide my hand from her belly to her breast and squeeze gently. She moans into my mouth, arching her back and pushing it into my hand. I run my thumb over her nipple.

When I shift to get her to lie down, the towel unwraps around my waist, leaving me naked as I lie alongside her. She slows our kiss and looks down at my now-hard cock.

"I just wanted to make sure you were actually able to get hard for me," she says, her hand venturing between my legs.

"Just so you stop second-guessing how fucking sexy you are." I get up on my knees and push away all the extra pillows. I run my hands up her legs, widening them.

"No, Damon. I didn't mean that."

"Spread for me, baby," I say, sliding to my stomach and bringing her legs over my shoulders. I cast a line of kisses along her inner thigh, shifting my attention from one leg to the other. "Still so fucking pretty."

I place a feather-light kiss on her clit, and her hips bolt off the mattress. I take her ass in both of my hands as I lick her and suck on her clit, rolling it around with my tongue.

"Oh god," she moans.

I squeeze her ass, bringing her pussy to my face as I lose myself in the taste of her. She's already writhing under me, and I've barely tasted her. I have a feeling her first orgasm is going to come quick because it's been so long, and she seems so damn sensitive. Thank fuck we're only doing this now under the guise of wanting to start labor because if we had started this earlier, I would've craved her every day damn I was living here. It's going to be hard enough to disentangle myself after today. If we'd been doing it for months, there would have been no chance.

I slide my hands under her dress and up under the edge of her bra until her tits are in my hands.

"Oh shit," she says, her hips rocking again. "Don't stop. Please… don't stop."

As if I ever would. My dick is so hard,

it's ready to explode without even being inside her.

She fucks my mouth, taking what she wants, and it's the sexiest thing I've ever seen. From being so shy moments ago to a sex kitten who isn't going to pass up this opportunity.

Adeline tries reaching to her side to pull my face off her pussy as her legs clamp around my face when she comes. She's crazy if she thinks I'm not going to ride this out with her. My tongue slows, concentrating little circles around her clit until she stops fighting me and her legs splay open, her hand falling to the mattress.

"I needed that so badly. Thank you," she pants.

I raise my head and push up her dress. Her shy face is back as I expose her belly. I sit on my knees, wrapping my hands around her bump, loving the feel of it in my hands. My baby is in there. *Our* baby is in there. I lean down and place a kiss on it. "I hope I don't scare him or her."

"Because you're so big?" she says dryly.

"Do I need to reacquaint you with him

again?" I move to lie at her side, then take her hand and place it on my rigid length.

"No, but good to know that ego is still in check."

"Sorry, but in the bedroom, my ego is at superhero level." I suck on her nipple, not giving her a chance to talk anymore.

"Oh shit. That is." She tugs at my dick as I place one hand on her tit while my mouth sucks, licks, and toys with her breast.

They're definitely bigger than I remember. She moans, getting a little rough with my cock, but she's loving this titty play. Since it's my favorite part of a woman, I don't mind giving hers the extra attention she's desperate for.

"Oh, Damon," she says, but stills.

Shit, is she having an orgasm from the titty play? Her body is so responsive, I can't get enough. Maybe I'm gonna have some kind of pregnancy kink now.

"Oh!" she screams, and I strip my mouth off her tit with a pop, feeling a gush of warm fluid around my legs.

I look down at the soaked sheets. "Either you squirted or…"

"My water just broke."

CHAPTER 14
ADELINE

"We can go a little faster, Damon." Despite my contractions, I wish I'd gotten in the driver's seat.

"I don't want to hurt you." He glances at me.

His sweatpants are still bulging from the fact he never got the relief I did. I can't believe we crossed that line, but damn, did I need that orgasm. The afterglow was the best I've felt in months.

"You know what's gonna hurt me? Your baby's head bearing down on my cervix, so press the gas, big guy." I grab my stomach as another contraction hits me, though it's not vicious, it's just very uncomfortable.

"Big guy, huh?" He smirks at me.

"Eyes on the road. And believe me, I'm already scared of how big this baby's head is going to be if it comes out with the same size ego you have."

"My mom never complained about my head." He stops at the red light.

"Good to know, but then again, you walk on water with her. Why are you stopped at the light? I'm in labor."

He looks both ways and accelerates. "You're very demanding."

"I thought for sure you'd be the kind of guy driving like you're an F1 driver, not an elderly man who can't see through his thick glasses."

"I'm just trying to be cautious. There could be drunk people on the road or teenagers speeding. I'm watching out for you and the baby." His voice is so sincere, I regret being hard on him.

"I'm sorry, thank you. I do appreciate it. But I want you to visualize pushing a human out of your nostril. You do not want to deliver our baby." He opens his mouth, but I continue. "I'm sure you're about to say something cocky, but really think about that for a moment."

He nods and presses on the gas again, weaving between cars. So, we're either one extreme or the other. At least this will get me to the hospital.

Pulling up to the emergency room when we reach the hospital, he gets out without putting his vehicle in park. Alarms go off as it starts to roll down the drive.

"Shit!" He runs back and catches the door before sliding in and pressing on the brake, then looks at me with an expression as though he thinks it's funny. "Sorry."

He puts his vehicle in park and exits again, helping me out of the passenger seat. I waddle behind him while he rushes into the hospital screaming, "My baby… woman having a baby!" over and over until an orderly comes out with a wheelchair.

"Hey, Damon Siska, right?"

Damon touches his head. No hat, which means even if he could get by without being recognized, there's no chance of that happening now.

"Yeah, man." He shakes the orderly's hand.

The orderly looks in my direction. "I heard something about this. This is your girl?"

I don't wait for him to answer before I sit in the wheelchair. "I'm just the baby mama."

Damon shakes his head at me with a grin because, though I don't know what exactly we are, we both know we're more than that to each other. I just let the man eat me while full term. That's not baby mama territory.

The orderly wheels me down the hallway while asking Damon questions about the upcoming season. "Think Rice's arm can handle another year? And what about Cavanaugh? Now that he's engaged, rumors are he's lost his appetite for the win."

"They'll both do great," Damon says.

"Adeline Morgan," I say when we reach the nurses' station.

A nurse walks around the counter. "Contractions?"

"Not terrible yet, and not really close together," I say.

"Has your water broken?"

"Oh, yeah," Damon answers for me, and we both laugh.

I wonder what these people must think.

The nurse looks at the orderly. "Let's get her up to labor and delivery. I'll call to let them know you're on your way."

"Thank you."

We move to wheel away, but she pushes a piece of paper and pen toward Damon. "Oh, Mr. Siska, could I bother you?"

I huff.

"Not at all." He scribbles his signature. "Have a great night."

"Good luck. Thank you."

Can't anyone see I'm having a baby here?

The nurse pats my arm. "You're beautiful, don't listen to those trolls online." She winks, and her gaze shifts to the orderly's. "Take her up, Jacob."

"Oh, she's so sweet," I say when we're in the elevator.

Damon steps in with us. "Really? Because when she asked for my autograph, you looked like you wanted to scratch her eyes out."

Labor and delivery is where it's at. The only downside is that they'll only let me eat ice chips.

"Bet you're wondering right now whether you should have gone for the pizza instead of the orgasm." Damon sits in a chair with a magazine that the orderly bought him from the gift shop. Of course Damon paid him back, but I wanted to ask: how about the woman with the baby inside her trying to get out?

"The orgasm was worth it, and if it spurred this little one to come out, it's all worth it."

"You make it sound like it was a sacrifice?" He lifts his gaze from the magazine. "Did I disappoint?"

I shake my head, my cheeks feeling hot again. "Of course not. I just meant letting you see me like that." I look around. "Naked," I whisper.

"I've seen you naked before," he whispers back.

"Not nine months pregnant," I whisper.

He shrugs. "It was sexy. You should own it. But if I'm going to be presentable, I need to think of something else." He stares between his legs.

"You're an ego inflator, thank you. And I'm sorry you didn't get yours." I bite my lip.

"I'm not just inflating your ego, I'm speaking the truth. And it's okay, you'll have time to pay me back." He closes the magazine. "Actually, it appears we have some time now. This is going pretty slow." He stands, grabbing the hem of his shirt. "My bare chest gets you all hot, right?"

"Damon," I say with zero fight in my voice.

"What?" He gives me wide, innocent eyes.

I don't know what this is, but I'm enjoying flirting with him.

He comes over to my bedside, takes my hand that isn't hooked to anything, and slides it under his T-shirt. God, his body is so impressive, so ripped, so strong. Leaning over me, he's millimeters from my lips, and my teeth bite harder on my lip.

"Set that lip free before I do it for you," he whispers.

My bottom lip pops out.

"There you are!" My mom walks in, and Damon slides back, turning around—trying to adjust himself, I think. "The orderly gave me the third degree. Accused me of being a reporter to get the juice on Damon."

"He's got a fan club here," I say, glancing at him.

Damon turns around. "You made good time." He sits back down, placing the magazine on his lap.

I chuckle to myself.

"I don't live far. What is with you two? You're acting odd."

"Nothing, Mom, it's just been hurry up and wait. We're bored and tired and hungry."

"Speaking of, why don't you go get some food for yourself, Damon? Call your parents." My mom takes off her coat and puts it and her purse on the chair next to him. "I'll take this shift."

"I'm not going anywhere," Damon says.

"She's not having this baby anytime

soon. Is she crying in pain?" My mom puts her hand out to say look at her.

"One of us should eat. You go." I motion toward the door.

He stands and grabs his sweatshirt. "You sure?"

"We'll call you if anything happens."

"All right." He comes over to the side of the bed, leaning down as if he's going to kiss me, but quickly turns and leaves.

As soon as he's out the door and we can no longer hear his footsteps, my mom says, "Did you sleep together?"

"No." I try to sound as though it's stupid of her to ask, but my mom knows me way too well.

"Liar. I warned you. If you two are going to be successful in this endeavor, you need to keep the physical stuff out of it."

"You make it sound like we're going on some space mission. And it was only to spur on labor. And if you want to get technical, there was no actual sex."

She crosses her arms and raises her eyebrows at me.

"You're my mom, and I do not want to talk to you about this."

She blows out a breath. "Just watch yourself. Sometimes babies make men grow up, but other times they don't. I have no reason to believe Damon is going to leave you high and dry at some point, but it's also not football season. I just don't want to see you get hurt because your expectations don't meet reality."

I hate the fact my mom is making me doubt him and what we did. Surely him going down on me earlier isn't going to affect our co-parenting. It's not as if I'm going to tell him how much I want to do it again after the doctor clears me for sex. The man knows his way around a woman, and he made me feel special and cared for tonight. It's the opposite of how I felt last August—wanton and liberated—but no less satisfying. There's absolutely no reason I can't compartmentalize this.

I hope.

My mom sits in the chair Damon just left.

"Where's Dad anyway?"

"In the waiting room. Said he's not taking any chances on seeing anything he's not supposed to." She picks up the magazine Damon left behind.

A doctor who is not Dr. Griffin walks into the room with the nurse who's been helping me. He scans the room before his attention lands on me. I want to point at myself and say, "Me, I'm the patient."

"I'm Dr. Porter, the doctor on call. You called Dr. Griffin and told her you were here, correct?"

I nod. "Yes."

"I'm sure she's en route then. I'm just going to do a quick exam to see if you're dilated." He glances at the machines I'm hooked up to. "Everything on the monitors looks good. How are the contractions?"

While I answer, he goes over to the sink and washes his hands. Putting on gloves, he looks around the room again, as if maybe he's missed Damon Siska, the Grizzlies wide receiver, being in here. Does he think Damon's hiding behind the curtain? As though he's going to pop out and yell surprise? Seriously, I'm getting annoyed.

The nurse puts my legs in the stirrups and glances between my legs. Maybe if I told him Damon Siska's tongue was just on my vagina, it'd make this doctor more eager to pay attention to me.

He takes a seat on the stool at the end of the bed, does his exam, and slides away, taking off his gloves. "You're a couple of centimeters dilated, so you have some time. I expect contractions to start getting worse. Did you want an epidural?"

What I want is Dr. Griffin. Not this man, who seems more worried about seeing my baby daddy than taking care of our actual baby.

"I think I want the epidural." Damon and I discussed it, and he agreed that it's ultimately my decision what route I want to go. I'd like to have the bragging point of being able to say I did it without the drugs, but I know my limits.

"Good choice. Especially if…" He looks around the room once again.

"Damon's not here, okay? He's in the building, and you'll probably see him at some point, but he's not hiding from you," my mom says. "And I can tell you one thing, he wouldn't be happy you're giving my daughter half your attention when it's *his* baby she's giving birth to." My mom crosses her arms and stares at the doctor.

I bite my cheek to keep from laughing. Guess I wasn't the only one who noticed.

"My apologies, it's just rare that… anyway, you are right." His cheeks are a little red now with embarrassment. Good. "I'm one hundred percent focused on you until Dr. Griffin gets here."

"The cafeteria sucks." Damon walks back into the room. "So, you're not missing anything." He's busy staring at his phone.

The doctor's jaw slowly opens, and his head falls back to look up at Damon since he probably has him by a foot.

"Damon, meet Dr. Porter. He's the interim until Dr. Griffin gets here," I say.

Damon looks up and stuffs his phone in his pocket. "Good to meet you. Everything is okay?" He looks at me instead of the doctor.

I give him a small smile and nod.

"Good, and our privacy is protected under HIPAA, right? I don't need you to sign an NDA?"

My head falls back on the pillow. Damon and his legal stuff.

"Of course, HIPPA protects you," Dr. Porter stutters, because now he seems seriously starstruck. Must be a big football fan, I guess.

"Good." Damon sits in the chair beside my mom.

And then the worst pain of my life contracts my uterus, and I shout in pain. Yup, I will definitely be getting that epidural.

CHAPTER 15

DAMON

The sound that flies out of Adeline's mouth makes it sound as if she's being eaten alive. I spring up from the chair, my phone dropping on the floor, and I rush to her side.

"This is normal. All good signs." Dr. Porter, who I can tell is more into me than his patient, smiles.

Adeline's eyes widen, and she arches her back, hands on her stomach. "Holy hell!" She looks at her mom with an expression of, "Is this really what this is like?"

Her mom nods with a smirk.

"Once you get a little further along, we can call for an epidural. Dr. Griffin should be here by then." Dr. Porter starts to leave the room, and I pull him back by the collar of his white jacket.

"Excuse me, you can't give her anything now? Didn't you just see how much pain she's in?"

He steps away to remove my hand from him. "This is called having a baby. I know it's her first one, but what did you both think it involved?"

"We don't need your sarcasm, and yes, this is *both* of our firsts." I emphasize both, so he knows it's my first baby too. "Some guidance would be nice. Like when can she get the epidural? How long will it take for her to dilate before she can start pushing?"

Her mom feeds Adeline ice chips. There's a line of sweat along Adeline's hairline now.

"If you're looking for specifics, I can't give them to you. Every birth is different. It's like a playbook. It doesn't execute the same way every time." He walks out of the room, and I follow, stopping the nurse in the hallway.

"Excuse me," I say, gently taking her elbow.

She swivels back around. "Do you need something else?"

"How do I help her?" I ask. "I can't just sit there, hold her hand, and feed her ice chips. There has to be something else I can do."

She smiles and even laughs a little. "Unfortunately, everything you just mentioned is exactly what you can do. If you want, she can try a hot shower or a bath, too. She'll have to deal with some pain, but try distracting her and make sure you encourage her. You'll get through it."

I nod, but I'm not really satisfied with her answer. "Thanks."

The whole time leading up to this point, there's always been something I can do—go to the appointments with her, paint the baby's room, drive her to and from work, make sure she's fed. Now the big moment is here, and I feel useless.

I head back into the room, and Adeline's head is listed to the side while her mom places a washcloth on her forehead.

How did I get here? Three months ago, I was single, carefree, and able to go anywhere I wanted. And now I'm begging some woman to tell me how to take the pain away from the woman I had a one-night stand with nine months ago so she can give birth to our child.

My thoughts travel to Greta. If things had been different, would I already be in this stage of life? Would we be married and have kids, living in some suburban home?

"I don't like him," Adeline says, drawing my attention. "I want Dr. Griffin. I do not want him to deliver our baby. The baby will feel all the tension in me, and he or she should only feel love."

"He said she should be on her way. I'll call her."

I grab my cell phone off the floor and dial Dr. Griffin as I walk into the hallway. She answers, but it's clear from the background noise that she's driving.

"Hello, Damon, I'm on my way. Just a little traffic to deal with. I was in the city at a play with my husband. But I talked to Dr. Porter, and he assured me that she's early in the process. She'll probably deliver sometime in the morning."

Morning? I search out a clock to see that

it's only seven o'clock at night. "Are you serious?"

She laughs. "Yes. Childbirth isn't usually a fast process, but we'll get there."

A horn honks in the background. "I'll let you concentrate on the road. Adeline will be happy you'll be here."

"I'll be there as soon as I can."

I walk back into the room to find Adeline in the middle of a contraction.

"She's on her way." I take her small hand, and she squeezes tightly. Holy shit, she's got some grip.

"OHHHHH… AHHHH…" She moans before switching to some breathing technique.

"Shouldn't we have done Lamaze?" I ask, and her mom gives me an expression like why bother asking about it now.

"I did… ah… videos online."

"And you didn't include me? I'm your partner. How am I supposed to keep you on track, be your coach?"

Adeline breathes fast, turning in my direction.

"I thought we were in this together?"

Her contraction must subside because she inhales one deep breath. "Shit, this is so different than cramps." She squeezes my hand. "Did you want to see a live birth? And honestly, it isn't like I'm saying no to the epidural."

"I guess so." I still don't feel great about it. How did I forget the whole Lamaze thing? It's in every damn movie.

Eventually, everything calms down for a while. Her mother and I slide chairs over to be closer to the bed. The hospital even calms down outside our doors. They've darkened the room, and less staff seem to be walking the floor.

I must've fallen asleep because I'm awoken by Adeline's hand running through my hair. It takes a second before I realize where we are and what we were doing.

My head shoots up with alarm. "What's wrong?"

"Nothing. Rarely do I ever see you so peaceful. We're having a baby." Her voice sounds wistful, almost like she can't believe it.

I smile at her and nod. "We are. Well, you are."

"Don't worry, once he or she is out,

you'll be doing your share." Again, her smile pierces my heart.

"Damn right."

We stare at one another for a while, and I wish I knew what was going on in her head. These past few months, we've grown close, and now we're going to raise a baby together.

I haven't had a moment to really think about what happened right before we left for the hospital, and I'm not sure now is the time.

"I'm here!" Dr. Griffin comes in. "Sorry, I stopped for a quick dinner. I was only down the street in case something happened fast, but I see we're stalling a little." She washes her hands and goes over to the machine that spits out paper.

The nurse follows and glances at Adeline and me.

"Although you two look really relaxed, how about we get you up and walking around, Adeline?" the doctor says.

"Seriously?" I can't keep the surprise from my voice.

"Oh, I could use it. I'm sick of lying down." Adeline is already trying to sit up.

"Where's your mom?" I ask, sounding a tad more alarmed than I probably should.

Adeline laughs. "She's with my dad. They were going to get something to eat before the cafeteria closed."

My eyes widen. "But she's our expert!"

Dr. Griffin's forehead wrinkles as she stares at me.

"I mean, she'll tell me what I should be doing." I haven't felt this helpless since that day with Greta. I hate hospitals.

"I'll be happy to direct you, Damon." Dr. Griffin smiles. "Okay, let's get you up."

She and the nurse help Adeline get unattached to the monitor while I put on her socks over her cute pink painted toenails that she got done with Sami the other night. Dr. Griffin and the nurse help Adeline out of bed and hand her over to me with matching grins.

And we walk down the hall.

And up the hall.

And back down the hall.

And up the hall again.

Adeline's labor starts up again and fast.

So fast that there's some guy here to give her an epidural. In the meantime, her mom still hasn't come back. I even sent her a text from Adeline's phone.

"You're used to holding things still, right? Cradling that football into the end zone?" The anesthesiologist's humor isn't really hitting tonight. "She has to stay still. Do you hear me, Adeline? You must stay still no matter what."

She nods and looks at me with her lips pursed. She's sitting on the side of the bed with her legs dangling between us.

Jesus, women go through a lot for a baby. I'd never admit it to anyone, but I'm happy it's not us guys who have to deal with all this stuff.

I hold her, her forearms gripping my upper arms, her head cradled in my neck. It's the first time I've seen her really afraid of anything.

"It's okay. I've got you," I whisper, and I'm not sure I even knew how much I meant that until right now. We're in this crazy situation, but I would never leave her to deal with this by herself.

The anesthesiologist pulls out the needle he's about to put in her back and I swallow as hard as I can.

"What? It's big, right?" Adeline says, pushing her forehead into my neck a little more.

"No. It's fine." I mean, it's not the needle that scares me as much as the fact the anesthesiologist looks as if he's about twelve.

"Okay, Adeline, I'm going to be putting the needle in," he says.

"Okay."

"Don't move," he repeats.

"She's got it. Can we just do it?" I ask with a bite to my tone.

"Distract me," she asks softly.

"Okay, um… your tits look great in that hospital gown."

"What?"

"Just kidding."

"The needle is in. Give me another minute, then you can lie back down," he says.

"You scared me," Adeline says.

"I couldn't make you laugh, and you gave me no time to think of anything to say. And hey, it would be nice to give the anesthesiologist a glimpse of his first breast."

She laughs and shakes her head.

I thought after the epidural, things

would speed along, but no, they slow down again. Until five o'clock in the morning, when it's time to start pushing.

"You're doing great, Adeline. Keep going. Another push."

Dr. Griffin, some nurses, and, thank God, her mom are here. I have one hand, and her mom has the other one.

"Daddy and Grandma, pull the legs," Dr. Griffin says.

"Legs?" I ask.

Her mom takes Adeline's leg and pulls it back toward Adeline's head. If I move her other leg, I'm going to see what's going on between her legs.

I copy her mom and divert all my attention away from the lower region.

"Count down from ten. Ready?" Dr. Griffin leads. "Ten... nine... eight... seven..."

Damn, Adeline's strong. Not once has she said she was done or too exhausted to finish. She's done everything Dr. Griffin said without argument, and I can see how much this is taking out of her.

"There you go," Dr. Griffin says. "Rest up for a moment, then we're going to go in again. The head is crowning, so we're almost there, okay?"

Adeline nods, sweat pouring down her face, her robe barely covering her.

"Daddy, support her back when she pushes. Help her crouch forward," Dr. Griffin says.

I nod, wishing I had eight hands to help her even more. I feel worthless here. She's doing all the hard work.

The doctor tells her to push again, and Adeline moves up, pushing. I place one hand on her upper back and use my other to hold her leg as I count down with everyone else in the room.

"The head is out. Stop for a moment," Dr. Griffin says.

My stomach does this weird swooping sensation. Whether it's excitement or nerves, I don't know.

"Beautiful," her mom says, and I want to look, but I'm not sure what to do.

Adeline somehow notices my trepidation because she's amazing like that. "Go ahead and look if you want."

I glimpse past her leg, and holy shit, a lot is going on down there. But I see a full head of dark hair, then Dr. Griffin does something and I hear our baby cry. Adeline smiles and lies back on the bed. I squeeze her hand as unshed tears clog my vision.

"Now let's push and get this baby out so he or she can meet their mama." Dr. Griffin cradles the head. "Okay, here comes another contraction, let's go again."

Adeline pushes, and her face turns red. She appears more determined than before.

"We've almost got the shoulders out. Let's keep going. Push again."

Barely getting a break, Adeline gets up, her movements slow, her fatigue showing, but she doesn't complain.

"You're doing great, baby. You're so strong," I whisper in her ear. "You're going to be the best mom, I just know it."

Our eyes lock for a moment right before the doctor says, "She's out! Congratulations, you two, you have a daughter." Dr. Griffin holds up our daughter for a moment.

"A girl?" Adeline smiles at me, then her mom.

"I'm gonna be a girl dad?" I ask in disbelief, overwhelmed by all the feelings rushing through me.

Adeline turns to me, tears filling her eyes. "And you'll be amazing."

A nurse places our daughter in Adeline's arms, and I wrap my arm around her shoulders, peering down at the most beautiful baby girl who ever existed in the history of the world.

CHAPTER 16
ADELINE

Clover Rose Siska loves her daddy.

We came home from the hospital two days ago, and she's already managed to wrap Damon around her finger.

I lean my shoulder against the nursery door frame, watching Damon pick up our little girl out of her crib and cradle her in his arms. He takes her to where he usually does—the lounger he found at the baby store that he was obsessed with. As he sits, he notices me in the doorway.

"I got this one. Go get some sleep."

I step in and sit gently on the floor, still a little tender. "I'm already up." Plus, I love watching him with her, but I won't say that.

I know I should be tired, but I feel as if I'm wired on some energy drink. My mom swears the exhaustion will come. It probably doesn't help that Damon's parents and brother are coming tomorrow to meet Clover. I'm nervous because I never used the interior designer, opting to do it with Damon. We actually make a pretty good team —better than I would have thought.

His eyes never leave Clover's. He's mastered the swaddle already, and I worry that maybe he's a more natural parent than I am. He even managed to figure out how to open that damn stroller with one hand.

"All the other parents think they have a beautiful baby, but that's just because they haven't seen ours," he says in what I've come to think of as his baby voice. He's smirking at Clover. God, I love that smirk.

"Good genes, I suppose."

"Mine might have won out a little more." He laughs and winks at me. Clover squirms in his arms as if she doesn't like him flirting with other women. "I'm kidding. She takes after her mommy, obviously."

I blush at his compliment.

"Oh, she's making those sucking lips," he says. "Good thing you woke up."

Now my anxiety ramps up. I've yet to be able to produce enough milk to breastfeed her, so I've had to supplement with formula.

I stand and head over to change positions with him, my heart already beating out of control from my nerves. He hands her to me, and we're still perfecting the exchange, so we laugh, not knowing which way the other person is going with their arms.

"I'll go make a bottle," he says and walks downstairs.

"Just you and me, baby girl." I rock her a little, but she's already arching for my breasts. "We can do this, right? One day soon I'll have enough for you."

It's the one area where I feel as if I'm failing us. I know how important it is to breastfeed. Everyone's been nice about it— the nurses and my mom and Damon especially—but I can't help but worry. They all said the more I stress, the worse it might become, but I cannot stop myself from fixating on it.

I unbutton my pajama blouse and slide

over one side of my bra. She attaches easily, and I relax in the chair as she suckles, but I never have that overfull feeling like I need to release milk.

Damon comes in with a warm bottle. "How's it going?"

"She'll probably start screaming in a second."

He gives me the same look as he always does. The small purse of his lips as if he's apologizing for the fact my body is failing us.

As I predicted, she stops sucking and cries. I pick her up and pat her back to get her to burp before we give her the bottle.

"If you want me to feed her, I can." Damon sets the bottle on the table next to the chair, and I catch him staring at my tit.

"What are you looking at?"

"You can't expect me not to look. Plus, I kind of wondered if it was going to look... different?" His gaze doesn't move from my breast.

"We're not doing that 'you get a taste' thing. Breast milk isn't your kink, is it?"

He shrugs. "I don't know. This is my first opportunity to find out."

"Damon!"

He chuckles, and Clover relaxes in my arms. She feeds off her dad's energy. I swear I think she's going to have his personality more than mine.

"I had to lighten up the mood. Adeline, everyone said there's nothing you can do. I was a formula baby, and look how I turned out." He holds his arms out at his sides. "You know how perfect I am."

I laugh. I always appreciate it when he lightens the mood.

When I lower Clover back down and feed her the bottle, she quickly starts sucking again. Damon takes my spot on the floor by the door, his back resting along the wall, his knees propped up as he watches her.

"Go back to bed," I say.

He shakes his head. There's something going on in that beautiful head of his that he's not sharing. I'm afraid to pry, afraid of what I might find out. So we sit in silence and feed our baby.

———

The next afternoon, Damon's sitting on the couch, Clover in her bassinet next to him, while he watches the Colts baseball game.

"We could be on the rooftop right now," he says absentmindedly, reminding me that he has a very different life than mine. At least he did. He's become so much a part of my life as of late, I can't imagine either of us just going back to our old ones.

"With Clover, I'm sure that would be fun," I say, arranging a veggie tray for his parents and brother, who will be here soon. I spent most of the morning making dips and appetizers. My mom is bringing over lasagna. His dad isn't my biggest fan, and now his brother is coming too, whom I've never met, so nervous doesn't aptly describe how I'm feeling.

"She'll grow up going to a lot of sporting events. I'm thinking by next year, she can go to a football game, right?"

"Sure, do you think they'll be okay with her being on the sidelines with you?"

I turn toward him, and he shakes his head. "Smartass."

"Do you want to hold a sixteen-month-old on your lap for an entire game?"

He stands and heads my way, grabs a carrot, dips it, and chomps down on it. "Give me some credit, I'd get a box for my girls." He winks.

"How sweet." I ignore the way my chest warms when he refers to Clover and me as his girls.

His hands land on my hips from behind me, and he leans down. "Relax, it's just my parents."

"Your very rich parents." I finish arranging the tray to my liking.

"Speaking of…" He stares out the front window. "They're here, honey," he says, in a voice as though we're a couple, and this is something we do all the time.

I'd feel so much better if my mom and dad were already here, but she's cooking the lasagna at her house, so mine won't be full of smoke if the sauce drips on the bottom of the oven.

Walking over, I see his family through the front window climbing out of a black SUV with tinted windows. "That's Ollie? Wow, you can tell you're brothers."

Damon scowls at me. "What did I ever do to you?" Then he opens the door.

His mom kisses his cheek and comes over and hugs me. "Hi, Adeline. Where is she?" She pulls away and scans behind me.

"The bassinet. She's sleeping."

Heather rushes over, stopping at the coffee table to put on some sanitizer from the bottle there, and she picks up Clover. Okay then.

"Oh my god, she's so beautiful," she coos. "Come look, Stanley."

"You're living here?" Ollie asks when he comes into the house.

"Yes, dipshit, and don't say anything," Damon says in a low voice, but I still hear him.

Ollie walks into the room. His entire persona screams, "I have money." His loafers and sweater have matching logos I'm not familiar with, but I'm sure they are some uber-expensive designer brand. His dark-blond hair is perfectly styled, not a hair out of place.

I definitely prefer my Siska.

Ollie holds up both hands. "Hey, I wasn't going to say anything. It's cute in here."

Damon mouths sorry at me and shuts the door.

"She's the most beautiful baby I've ever seen," Stanley says, having bypassed me and gone straight over to the baby.

I'm not sure if Heather is going to give her up or if Stanley even wants to hold her.

"Ollie, come look at your niece," Heather says.

He walks over and peers into his mom's arms. "She's too pretty to be Damon's." He laughs and comes over to the table. "Catered or homemade?"

Seriously, this guy is a dick.

"Homemade. You'll have to slum it." I give him my best version of a serene smile.

Ollie laughs at me, pointing his half-eaten green pepper my way. "I like you. I bet you give him a run for his money. He needs that. God knows from what I heard, Greta never did it."

Greta? Who's Greta?

The doorbell rings, and I'm thankful to see my mom in the window.

Damon opens the door, and she shoves the covered lasagna with a towel on the bottom into his hands. "Warm it until we're ready to eat."

My dad follows her in with fresh

bakery bread in hand, and he and Damon go into the kitchen. My mom rushes over to sit by Heather on the couch, putting hand sanitizer on as if telling Heather my turn. Unable to deal with that, I go into the kitchen.

"We've got this. Go enjoy our company." Damon puts the oven on warm and places the lasagna inside.

"It's almost her feeding time," I say, warming a bottle to keep myself out of that room.

I'm not a huge fan of his dad, and now I've added his brother to my shit list.

But the bottle doesn't take long to get ready. I'm still struggling through this breastfeeding thing, but I'm pumping as much as I can and supplementing with formula.

I go into my family room and sit in the chair.

"Bottles?" Heather asks, and I open my mouth, hoping I can answer without animosity.

"Yeah, Adeline works, and I really want to feed the baby too. We decided this is what's best for us," Damon says.

I look at him, wondering why he told her that. To protect my feelings?

"Look at Mr. Domestic here. Maybe you can get a pair of fake tits to wear to feed the baby, like in that one movie." Ollie laughs, and Stanley stares at him as though he's ready to murder his youngest son.

"I didn't breastfeed. I had Damon early, he couldn't attach, and my milk just never came in." Heather gives me a sympathetic look, as if she knows her son well enough to know he made up an excuse for me and doesn't want me to feel bad.

"Damon, not knowing what to do with a nipple? He sure made up for lost time with that." Ollie again can't read the room because no one laughs at his joke.

"And Ollie was so feisty, I was afraid to let him near my nipple," Heather says, giving her son a pointed glare.

Damon laughs hysterically and shoves his brother into the wall when he walks by him toward the food.

"So, you're living here?" Stanley asks Damon.

"Yep," Damon says, keeping his voice light.

"And the apartment downtown?" His dad arches an eyebrow, and it reminds me of how I've seen Damon do the same a time or two.

"I still have it. I'll have to live there during the season. The commute would kill me."

I've been so occupied with Clover that I haven't thought that far ahead. In the days since Clover has been home, I've only been thinking hour by hour. I haven't thought about what happens when Damon starts playing again. When he's traveling to out-of-town games.

I stare at Clover in Heather's arms, and realization washes over me like a warm shower. I'm basically a single mother. Damon and I aren't a couple. He's going to start the season, sleep with women, and go out to clubs. He'll see Clover on maybe his one day off during the week, and we're going to coexist as Clover's parents who are not together.

These past few months are not our reality. We've been in our own little bubble, and I've grown way too used to Damon being here with me, forgetting that in a couple of months, it will all be on me.

Every one of those insecurities I had when I first found out I was pregnant flood back. Only this time, I know what I'll be missing.

CHAPTER 17

DAMON

TRAINING CAMP - TWO MONTHS LATER

"I can't believe you didn't bring your game console. You always bring it. What the hell?" Cooper pouts in the chair next to me in the lounge after another long day of training camp.

"I came straight from Adeline's house." I shrug.

That might not have been my wisest decision, but I just couldn't leave them. Even now, I've been here for two weeks, and I'm desperate to hold Clover again. But I keep that fact to myself, not wanting to give the guys anything to bust my balls about.

"Last I checked, either of you two could go out and buy another one," Miles says, lowering his reading glasses as if he's schooling us.

"That's a waste of money," Cooper says. "And this one has diapers and formula to buy."

Jackass.

"Bryce is coming this weekend," Miles says. "You should invite Adeline. Bryce really wants to meet her—officially."

"So does Ellery. Not to mention, we want to meet Clover. Tell me your brother isn't going to be her godfather?" Cooper puts his legs up on the table and tosses the playbook next to his feet. I'd hate to be the fucking quarterback.

"I don't even know if we're having godparents. Do you think you'd be the godfather if we were?" I ask Cooper.

"I'm happy being the honorary uncle," Miles says. "I've got my nephew now, and I'm his godfather."

I'd be happy with either of them being Clover's godfather or honorary uncle, but I haven't talked to Adeline about any of that yet.

"Let's get back to when Adeline's coming downtown." Cooper's shit-eating grin is annoying.

That's a long day for Clover, or if she spends the night, it's a lot of shit to pack for one night, and I haven't gotten anything set up for Clover at my place yet. I FaceTime them every night, and that's enough for the time being.

"There's too much press around here. Plus, the fans are all up in my business. I'm getting enough questions about the two of them. I don't want to expose either of them to that." I miss the little bubble we had at Adeline's.

"What are your plans for the season?" Miles asks. "Maybe you should talk to Jones or Miller, they're new dads."

"Oh, you could all join a club." Cooper laughs.

"I wish I had my game console just so you'd shut you the fuck up." I leave the room, sliding by some other players coming in.

I'm about to head to my room when

Ronnie Michaels, our GM, whistles and waves me down the hall. Great.

I follow him into his office here at Halas Hall, where training camp takes place, and he sits on the couch. The man never wears shoes and always has on funky socks. These socks have a dog's face on them. He catches me looking and wiggles his toes. "My kids got them for me. They're our dog's face. Wife got the dog in the divorce, so they thought I'd miss seeing him."

I nod. "Nice of them."

"Listen, Siska, I've been meaning to talk to you. As your general manager, I feel as if it's my duty to provide you some guidance on this new life path you're on. You got a woman pregnant from a one-night stand… you're not the first in the league, and you're not gonna be the last. But this whole hiding-out thing isn't going to work. The more you hide, the more the press and everyone else wants to find out."

"I'm not hiding. Adeline just doesn't live in the city, and the press doesn't come out to where she is. The town itself, surprisingly, has enough respect for us that we're rarely photographed."

Being in Adeline's small town was nice. At first, me being there was a novelty, but even before I came to training camp, we'd take walks with Clover, and people would wave hello and carry on their way. Sure, there was always the one guy or kid who asked me about the league, or the nosy person who wanted to see Clover, but that was far and few between.

"Family day is this weekend, and I think you should consider inviting them."

PR does a great job of arranging games and things for the kids, but this is not the year for me to bring her. Clover will come in maybe two years.

"Yeah, Clover is basically a newborn still. I'm not asking Adeline to do that. And honestly, I couldn't give a shit what the press wants."

Ronnie stares at me for an uncomfortable minute. "Okay, it was just a suggestion. Are you going to stay out in no man's land forever or return to the land of the living?"

"Boy, I can't imagine why you're divorced," I say, instantly regretting talking to him like that.

Rumor is Ronnie's wife wanted to move

out to the suburbs for the kids, and he didn't. It was one of many reasons why they got divorced. But my frustration has nothing to do with him, so I shouldn't take it out on him either.

"You never even married your baby mama, so I don't want to hear it. You have no idea what marriage is." He laughs, then starts telling me some story.

I zone out. There was a time when I thought marriage would be for me. A time when my mind roamed to imagining a woman in white walking down the aisle to me. But that was a long time ago.

I enjoy Adeline. We're almost like best friends.

Huh. Maybe the whole Ellery and Cooper thing makes more sense now. Then again, it's the way Cooper looks at Ellery as though she's his fucking world. Yeah, Adeline and I are rocking this whole living together-slash-co-parenting thing, but I can't let her become my whole world.

"She was sucking me off, and bam, I was cool being divorced."

I'm fairly sure I missed the point Ronnie was trying to make with his story, but no matter. Now all I can think of is how nice it would be to have my cock sucked. But the idea of going out to find some woman to hook up with doesn't hold any appeal to me.

Now if it were Adeline… I've been kind of hoping she'd be up for messing around again once she got cleared by the doctor, but thus far, she's indicated no interest in repeating what we did right before she delivered.

"Thanks for sharing. Oh, and we appreciate the team basket. Flowers were beautiful." Adeline had wanted me to thank them.

"You're welcome, but your baby mama already sent a thank you card three weeks ago. She's a good one. Don't fuck it up."

"I can't. We're not a couple." I stand from the couch.

"All right, here's my last piece of advice. The season is hard, as you know. You're traveling, you're training, you're practicing. There isn't a lot of free time. If you really want to be close to your daughter, find a way to get her down here. With your schedule during the season, you can't be commuting out there with the cows."

"Thanks, funny man." I walk to the door.

"Plus, I've been told you should have done more training in the offseason. Your conditioning wasn't up to snuff. You're lucky your GM is such a nice guy and understands you just had your first baby." He winks.

Disappointment washes over me. I did what I could before Adeline was born, but afterward, I just couldn't do as much as I wanted. Well, I guess I could have, but that would have meant not being there to support Adeline and my newborn daughter.

"Thanks, Ronnie." I knock on the door frame as a goodbye and leave.

His words haunt me as I walk to my room. I'm due to review film in an hour, so I figure I'll sneak in a FaceTime call to Adeline before I do that.

Adeline's face lights up the screen. "Hey! Oh wait, it's not me you want to see."

She puts the phone in front of Clover, and damn, my heart skips a beat as soon as her adorable face comes on the screen. I love her so much it hurts. Like a literal ache in my chest.

"Hey, girlie."

I smile wide at her, and Clover smiles back. I don't care what anyone says, it's not gas. Then she wiggles on the blanket Adeline has set on the carpet underneath her. Adeline's fingers tiptoe up her chest, and Clover makes that sweet cooing sound I love so much. My chest squeezes because I'm not there.

What is wrong with me? Football has always been my life. Number one, never questioned. Sure, I love my parents and my family, well maybe not Ollie as much—he has some growing up to do—but I've always wanted to be playing, always put it above anything and anyone else, and now this eleven-pound beauty owns me.

"Hey, do you think we can talk when I get back? Maybe you could come down to the apartment?" I ask.

"You want me to return to the scene of the crime?" She laughs and turns the camera to face her, as if I didn't know she's joking. "Why?"

"I figure it's about time you officially meet my friends, and I'll have to stay there more. I'll send a car for you."

"I can drive. Are you okay?" She frowns. "You seem… different."

"Just tired. Camp really works me hard, especially since I slacked a little during off-season." I smack on my best convincing smile, but I'd be lying if I said that what Ronnie said hasn't gotten my mind twisted up. That, and being away from the two of them.

"Okay, just give me the time and day. Not like I have a lot of plans for the rest of the summer. I did want to talk to you about what we're going to do when school starts up again though. Probably time to start adulting."

I laugh. "Fuck, I've done more adulting in the last six months than any other time in my life."

She shakes her head. "You wanna wait for tonight or do it now?"

"Let's do it now. There's no one here, and I don't want to listen to their shit if they find out what I do every night."

She makes a tsk sound. "Damon, it's sweet. Do you know how many women's ovaries would explode if they could watch you do it?"

I only care about one woman's, but I can't tell her that. "Yeah, yeah."

"Let me get her ready." She puts down the phone, and I dig into my suitcase to grab what I need on my end.

"Okay, Daddy's here again."

Clover's face comes into view again, and now she's in her bouncy seat, eyes wide open.

"Ready?" I open the book. "I love Daddy…"

I read the entire book while Adeline is nice enough to turn the pages on her end. It's something I asked if she'd be willing to do before I left. Of course, Adeline's such a rockstar, she agreed without hesitation.

"Good night, baby girl. I love you so much." I blow her a kiss. "Thanks, Adeline."

"Of course. I'll read 'I Love Mommy' twice tonight." She laughs. "It'll be a race to see which she says first, daddy or mommy?"

"Oh, you want to make a wager?" I waggle my eyebrows.

She laughs. "Nah, I saw it the minute you held her. A million hearts were breaking all over the country—a female finally owned Damon Siska's heart."

She's exactly right. But I was pretty fond of Clover's mom too. I'll keep that part to myself though.

CHAPTER 18
ADELINE

have to be honest, I hate driving into the city. I should have let Damon hire me a car like he offered. Clover was awesome on the drive down here though, since I tried to schedule it around her nap time.

Damon got home from training camp last night and is waiting for us to arrive at "The Den." I wasn't sure what it would be like to be here again. I park in the garage Damon instructed me to, and it's clear the attendant was already expecting us.

After getting Clover and her car carrier and the diaper bag, I go across the street. Thank goodness there isn't a Colts game to-day. That would be weird.

When I ring the buzzer, Damon answers, and I tell him it's us. Butterflies flutter in my stomach when the gate clicks open because it's been three and a half weeks since I've seen him face-to-face. Three and a half weeks since our private bubble was pried open by a crowbar with the responsibilities of the real world.

I climb the stairs, Clover making sounds that make me think she somehow knows we're about to see her daddy. I slow my movements, taking my time, trying to come to terms with the fact that I missed him. The worst thing I could do is catapult myself onto Damon when he opens the door. It's Clover he wants to see, not me. I'm just the tagalong, and I'm best to remember that.

I reach his landing, relieved to set down Clover's carrier. I face her toward the door and ring the bell, but I hear two sets of voices from down the stairs the minute I do. They grow nearer, then a shadow casts down over us. I turn to look over my shoulder and see Miles Cavanagh staring at me with astonishment.

A dark-haired woman I recognize from

TV as his fiancée runs into his back, almost falling down the concrete steps, but she grabs the railing. "Shit, you're lucky I didn't fall and somersault down these stairs."

I briefly met Damon's friends, except for Miles, the day we hooked up, but it was just in passing.

"Hi," Miles says.

"Hi," I say in return as Damon opens the door.

"Hi, guys," he says.

"Hi," they say in unison, obviously feeling uncomfortable and probably waiting for an introduction. I wouldn't mind one either.

"Come on in," Damon says to me.

I pick up the carrier, and Damon takes Clover from me, opening the door a little wider to let us in. I walk into his apartment, and he shuts the door. Miles laughs on the other side, but I have no idea why. Does he know something I don't? Why didn't Damon introduce us?

I follow him into his sitting area. The black leather sofas still make me laugh. He puts Clover's carrier on the coffee table and unbuckles her, lifts her out, and cradles her to his chest.

Damon leans his head down and inhales a deep breath against her hair. "Damn, I missed you."

My heart pitter-patters in my chest. Jeez, I cannot be jealous of my daughter, that would be pathetic.

"She's so big. How much has she grown?" he asks, holding her out in front of him. "And she's holding her head up." He sits on the couch, sulking.

"She hasn't grown that much. It's only been three and a half weeks, Damon." I sit in the chair, crossing my legs.

He's wearing a pair of shorts and a Grizzlies T-shirt, his skin more tanned from his outdoor practices than when he was at my house.

"How was training camp?" I ask.

"Lonely," he says without missing a beat.

I laugh. "Should I have called your cell phone at two in the morning? You could've done the night feedings with me."

He doesn't laugh. In fact, he frowns. "I'm sorry."

"Damon! Stop it. I'm only kidding.

What's wrong with you? It's your job, you have to go to training camp. How are you ever going to get through the season?"

I don't know much about professional football schedules, but I have to think they're demanding. For sure he'll be out of town for half his games, and although he doesn't play on Thanksgiving this year, he plays on Christmas Eve and New Year's Eve. His only week off is the first week of December.

It's ridiculous that I know his schedule better than he probably does.

He looks at Clover again, and God, the love in his eyes is so intense. I'm not sure I ever would've imagined Damon Siska could love so hard.

"I don't know how I'm gonna do it. It was hard being away from you guys. Maybe I should've asked you to bring her down, but that's a long drive, and I felt bad."

"I would have. My mom and dad could've come." In truth, I figured he wanted to do his own thing. Wanted to be free of the handcuffs our lifestyle put on him. Not that I thought he was out partying and sleeping with people—and even if he did, I have no say in that—but I'm surprised to hear how much being away from us has affected him. He put on a brave face whenever he called us from training camp.

"Yeah," he says, sounding lost somewhere in his mind.

"Talk to me. We're in this together," I say.

"First, I think she needs changing." He moves his head to the side to breathe.

"Yeah, for such a little thing, she sure can make a poop." I grab the diaper bag, but he places his hand over mine.

"There's something I want to show you." He stands and leads me to a room I wasn't in the night I was here. His bedroom and kitchen counter were the main spots I remember from that night.

"What is it?"

When we reach the door, he turns to face me. "I wanted to wait until later, but I can't. I'm just not the type of guy who can sit on something for days and hide it to make it some big thing."

I'm so confused, but I follow him into the room. He flicks on the light, and there's a queen-sized bed in one corner and a crib in the other with a changing table.

"This is beautiful," I say, my heart cracking. It only makes it more real that Clover won't spend all of her time with me. She's going to go back and forth between us at some point.

"I had Mom's designer do it while I was at camp. I figured Clover needed to have a place here too."

"Definitely." My voice trembles, and I hope he didn't hear it.

He takes the baby over to the changing table and undresses her to change her diaper. I'm not sure if he watched a YouTube video or what, but the man can change her better than me, which irritates me to no end. I'll give Damon one thing—as soon as he finds something to be a challenge, he does whatever he has to in order to conquer it.

"So, I was talking to my GM, Ronnie Michaels, and we were chatting about how I won't be as available to you during the season."

I sit on the edge of the bed. Here we go. The closet is partially open, and I see that it's full of clothes for Clover. I rise and walk over. "Yeah."

There's no way he's going to ask for partial custody, right? I didn't think we were at this point yet, although I guess we should be.

He's your one-night stand, not your boyfriend. Of course we're here.

I watch as he picks her up off the changing table. She always looks so much smaller when he holds her against his big body. I turn back to the closet, sliding the clothes carefully hung up on hangers across the bar.

"That's my mom's doing."

He sounds annoyed, but how could he be? Every item in here is probably from an upscale store I could never afford. Clover will be dressed in Target with me and a brand I probably can't even pronounce when she's with Damon. I'm sure the press will have something to say about that.

"It's all really nice," I say.

"Why would you put a baby in half that shit? I mean, she needs cotton on her skin." He looks at Clover and morphs into his baby voice. "Right, sweetie? Nice, soft cotton, not some itchy fabric."

I chuckle and shake my head. "You want her to dress like you?" My eyes float down his body. His strong chest and narrow waist and thighs that are so muscular they make my mouth water. It's so unfair that I have to know exactly what's under those shorts *and* how well he knows how to use it. "She's a girl, Damon."

"She's a baby." He walks out of the room. "Are you hungry?"

"Are you ever going to put her down?" I follow him into the kitchen.

He opens the fridge and pulls out some sushi. "Since you're not pregnant… at least, I assume you're not pregnant."

I tilt my head and huff.

He chuckles. "Just making sure." He leans in close to me. "And to answer your question, no, I'm never putting her down. Now you eat and relax."

He sits on the stool across from me, and I open the containers of sushi before grabbing a pair of chopsticks. I haven't had sushi since before I was pregnant, and after the long drive, I'm eager to eat.

"So, what do you think?" he asks.

I chew my first piece, covering my mouth and giving him a thumbs-up.

"Not about the sushi. The room?"

I swallow and take a sip of the water he gave me. "It's really nice. I'm sure she'll love it. How soundproof are the walls? Will Cooper and Miles be bothered by her crying?"

His eyebrows crinkle. "They won't hear her, and I'm pretty sure she doesn't give a shit where she sleeps, but what about you?"

I place the chopsticks down and wipe my mouth. "What exactly are you asking me, Damon?" I raise my water to take another sip.

"I want you to move in with me."

I spit the water all over the counter. "Shit, I'm sorry." I hurry and grab some paper towels. "Sorry. You surprised me."

He looks a little sheepish. "I probably could've set that up better. It's just that I won't have time to drive out to you every day, as much as I want to, and then there's the games on weekends. I'm off one day a week, but to see her only that one day… I know I'm asking a lot. You can say no, and I won't be upset, but I couldn't not ask."

"Um… I don't know how that would work…"

"I thought maybe you could move in

here during my season. Then, after the season, I'll find a place out by you. I know you'll have to commute to school, and I'll get you a driver. That way you can do whatever you have to during the drive. Hell, you could sleep there and back. But it's the only solution I can think of. I can get in late on some nights. Am I asking too much?"

Clover cries, and I'm not sure if it's because she doesn't have Daddy's attention or if she needs something.

"Is she hungry?" he asks me, rocking her gently.

"She could be." I move to stand, but he beats me to it.

"I made her two bottles already." He opens the fridge, and I want to cry. All these signs that one day we're going to have her stuff at his place and her stuff at my place. I hate it.

He continues talking as he warms the bottle, going on and on about how he's probably overstepped and didn't mean to, it's just that she's changing so fast and he's missing it.

I understand what he's saying. My mind continues to go to a time in the future when

I ring his doorbell with Clover's hand in mine and he opens the door for her to jump into his arms. Giving her a hug and telling her to have a great weekend. And then vice versa. Her leaving something at one of our houses and us trying to figure out how to get it to the other. And what if Damon does find a woman he wants to settle down with one day? Then I'll have to share Clover with even more people.

My throat closes up. I'll do anything to postpone that happening. "I'll do it."

He turns around and places the bottle in Clover's mouth, eyes wide. "Really?"

I nod.

The pure joy in his smile almost makes it worth knowing it'll hurt like hell when we finally do have to disentangle our lives. "Damn, thanks, Adeline. I really appreciate it. Whatever you need to make it easier, you name it."

"We'll figure it out."

"Yeah, we will." He smiles and walks into the living room with Clover in his arms.

I pick up the chopsticks, thinking I should stab my eyes out with them right now. How stupid can I be? I've agreed to live with the man who is my daughter's father and who I've been crushing on for months.

Stupid, Adeline, just stupid. You might as well take your heart out now and stomp all over it.

CHAPTER 19
DAMON

deline and Clover moved in with me last night, and I still feel as though I'm on a fucking high. Adeline's organizing things in her room while I play with Clover on what will be my last available weekend for a while. Tomorrow is D-day, and we both start our work schedules. I'm excited about the new season, but I'm dreading it at the same time.

After a while, Adeline comes in looking all cute with a scarf thing in her hair to keep it back from her face. She's wearing tight yoga pants and a small top that reveals a little of her stomach when she lifts her arms.

She's pretty much lost all of her baby weight, and I'm starting to realize that this whole moving in together thing is going to be harder on my self-control than I first thought. I haven't gotten laid in months. The last time I even came close was the night Clover was born. My hand is tired, and I'm desperate for a little action.

"So, my mom is good to help with Clover this week, but I think we need to discuss the nanny situation." She sits in the chair. I love how she constantly looks at my black leather furniture as though she wants to strike a match and set it on fire.

"I called an agency. They can send over applicants. I was thinking Tuesday evening?"

"Perfect. Thanks for taking the lead on that. My mind has been so occupied with my return to the classroom." She sips her water. "I'm not sure I'm gonna survive an entire day without her."

Her eyes tear up again. This has pretty much been her the entire past week.

"I'm just checking, but you're the kind of woman who wants to work, right?"

Her head tilts to the side, and her eyes

narrow a bit. "I'm curious, if I didn't work, how would I support myself and my daughter?"

Damn it, why can't I keep my mouth shut?

"I'd pay child support, of course."

She purses her lips with a pissed-off expression I haven't seen yet. "So I'd live with you and our daughter, and you'd pay me child support so I could sit around?"

I hate the way she poses it as a question as if I'm stupid. Maybe I am stupid for bringing this up. "I just want you to be happy, and if you want to stay home, I have the means to make it happen."

She shakes her head. "No, Damon, I'm happy to work. I am going to miss this little one so much." She swipes her out of my arms and blows a raspberry into Clover's neck while she circles the room. "But I know my place in this family of ours."

"Which is?" I watch her with Clover and try to ignore the warmth invading my heart.

She pretends they're dancing and taps Clover's nose before touching their two noses together. "I'm worth the least."

"Not a chance. What's that supposed to mean?" I scowl at Adeline.

She looks at me. "My daughter has a trust fund worth who knows how much." She quickly raises her hand. "And I don't want to know. That's between the Siskas. I'm a Morgan."

Her words leave a sour taste in my mouth. I'm done with this conversation.

"Forget unpacking, let's go for a walk." I stand from the couch. "Let's go to eat and spend our last day with her." I don't want to sit here and be upset. Tons of parents everywhere have to leave their kids to go to work.

"I look like crap." She scrunches up her nose.

"So? I don't look great." I'm only wearing shorts and a T-shirt.

"You're Damon Siska, and I'm the girl you knocked up. We'll be seen very differently by the outside world."

She's done better about not caring what she reads online, but I've noticed there are still times when it gets to her.

I wrap my arms around her and Clover. It feels so natural, so right. It must be because we share a daughter. "Tell Mommy how beautiful she is, and all the other women are jealous."

She looks at Clover. "Tell Daddy he lives in a fairy tale land."

"Come on, I know a great pizza place."

"Who doesn't know a great pizza place in Chicago?" she deadpans.

"You're lucky I love that smart mouth." I point at her and grab Clover, then put her in the carrier. "We're going. Are you coming?"

She stares at me as if testing me. "Fine. Let me get my shoes. But if I end up as on-line fodder, I'm going to kill you."

"Then you'll never see your daughter."

She makes an angry growl and meets me at the door after grabbing her diaper bag/purse combo she wears across her chest and between her tits, which makes the curves of them even more ample. God help me.

We reach the bottom of our stairs, and I'm attaching the carrier to the stroller when someone calls my name.

"And it already begins," Adeline grumbles.

"No, it's not the press." I turn around to see my foursome friend group walking toward us. "Guys." I nod at them, knowing the moment I've been putting off is finally here.

Adeline

"You finally came out of hiding." Cooper Rice pushes Damon's shoulder. "About fucking time." He turns his attention to me.

Shit, he is attractive. I mean, he does nothing for me, but his dark hair and those deep-set eyes aren't exactly a turn-off.

"I'm Cooper Rice." He puts his hand out between us. "Adeline, I assume."

"Of course it's Adeline, dipshit," Damon says. He seems tense that his friends are here, which I don't understand.

I shake his hand. "I know who you are, and it's a pleasure to meet you."

"I'm Ellery, Cooper and Bryce's best friend." A cute, long-haired blond pushes past Cooper and puts her hand out for me to take.

"Hi." I return her genuine smile.

"And you met Miles and Bryce the other

day," Damon says. "We're leaving, see you later." He starts to push the stroller, but I place a hand on his forearm to stop him.

"We said hi, and you slammed the door in our faces." Miles steps up and puts out his massive hand.

I shake it and smile, saying hello.

"Don't be a dick, Damon. It's about time we meet Adeline. You've been keeping her to yourself for too long."

I laugh at Bryce's attitude.

"Hi, Adeline, we're all gonna have a lot of fun while they're playing this year." Bryce turns toward Damon. "Which means you need to get her a season ticket by us so we can all sit together."

"Sure, I'll get right on that." He rolls his eyes.

"Now that we all know each other—wait, I haven't met my goddaughter yet." Cooper tries to see into the stroller, but Damon slams down the shade.

"Goddaughter?" My forehead wrinkles.

Damon turns to me. "I didn't tell you because it's not happening, but Coop put his hat in for godfather."

Cooper puts his arm around my shoulders. "Come on, I'm definitely a better option than Ollie."

I nod. "Who isn't?"

Cooper laughs. "I love you already. Now, why are you hiding the baby?"

I turn to Damon. "Yeah, why are you?" I whisper. I can't figure out why he's being this way.

"Because then we're inviting them into our life," Damon whispers back.

"They're your friends, are they not?"

Damon looks back and must realize I have a point. It's kind of sweet how he didn't really want them to poke their heads into our life, but the bubble we've put ourselves in can't stay like that forever.

"Fine. Clover, meet Daddy's dipshit friends." He lifts the shade.

All four of them descend on the stroller, fighting for face time.

"Oh my god, she's adorable," Ellery says. "Vaginal birth, right? How many hours were you in labor?"

"Um..."

"Told you," Damon says with raised eyebrows.

"Sorry, I'm a doctor. She really is in the

top ten of the cutest babies I've seen, and I wouldn't lie about that."

"Top ten. Fuck off. She's number one," Damon says.

"Thank goodness she looks like Adeline and doesn't have this ugly mug." Cooper slaps Damon on the back, obviously trying to start some kind of brotherly fight.

"Gorgeous." Bryce smiles at me.

Miles nods, gazing at his fiancée. "Let's have one."

"Cavanaugh, this is not something we decide by looking at one baby, but it's tempting," Bryce says.

Damon and I look at one another. I wonder if he's thinking the same thing as me. They have no idea what it takes. It's cute how she's content right now, but the other night when she was screaming bloody murder and we couldn't figure out why, not so much.

"Where are you guys going?" Ellery asks.

"Pizza," I answer as Damon says, "Nowhere."

"We could eat. Let's go." Cooper nods for us to walk ahead.

Damon groans but starts walking, knowing we don't really have a choice.

———

We're all seated at a popular pizza place at a round table with the stroller by me and Damon in the corner. Clover's sleeping, and I really hope she stays that way. This is the first time we've had her out at a restaurant.

"So, when can we take you out?" Bryce asks with a wide grin.

"Let me check my schedule." Ellery pulls out her phone.

"You're not taking her out. She has friends." Damon picks up the menu, even though I'm fairly sure he knows what he's having. On the walk over, he mentioned that he comes here a lot.

"She can have more friends," Bryce says.

I reach under the table and pinch Damon's leg.

He retracts it and leans in close. "Tell me you missed your mark."

"Stop being a dick. I want to get to know your friends."

"They're all trouble. They're going to say shit about me."

It's then I see the insecurity in his eyes, and I squeeze his knee before retracting my hand. "Damon, I know everything about you. It's not like I thought you were a saint. Hello, I got pregnant from our one-night stand."

He blows out a breath and sighs, then looks at the girls. "Fine, she can go out with you two."

I roll my eyes.

"Well, thank you. I mean, what would Adeline do if you didn't give her permission?" Ellery groans.

We set a date for when Damon will be home to watch Clover, and as if she heard her name, she whimpers in the stroller. I slide out of my chair, but Damon stands and picks her up, bringing her to sit with him at the table.

"Damn," Bryce says. "Even Damon looks good with a baby in his arms. Pass her off to Miles, I wanna see." She moves her finger as if she's directing a play.

"Screw off, she's my daughter, not a hot potato." Damon scowls at her.

I laugh. "They have a special bond."

He plays with Clover's pacifier, moving it closer so she opens her mouth, then away from her. She loves it, but he eventually gives it to her and whispers, "Good girl," in her ear. I have to suppress a shiver when I think of how I'd like to hear him whisper the same thing to me.

"Oh shit," Ellery says. "You're changing my opinion about you having a baby."

"Really, this is adorable, but it's not always like this," I say.

Damon puts his free arm around the back of my chair. "What are you talking about? It's great."

I give him a doubtful look. "Sometimes."

The pizza comes, and we pass Clover back and forth while we eat, but Bryce finishes before any of us and demands to take Clover so we can both eat.

"Give her the baby," I say to Damon, who is holding her hostage.

"I can hold a baby, Damon. I need practice in case Miles and I have one."

Miles's eyes widen. "Shit, that was fast. I want her pregnant with my baby. Give her the baby, Siska."

Miles isn't really what you'd expect of a professional athlete. Or maybe he just loves Bryce so much he's not afraid to tell the world.

Finally, Damon hands Clover over, being bossy on how to put her arms, telling Bryce he'll place the baby in her arms and she's just not to move.

"I'm sorry," I say, apologizing for his behavior.

"Believe me, I'd rather have this version of Damon than the other one," she says.

"Other one?" I ask.

"Before you." Bryce smiles and hugs Clover to her body after Damon releases her.

"Yeah, I can't believe how much you've changed, Siska," Cooper adds.

"Amazing what a baby can do," Miles says and smiles at Bryce holding Clover.

I force a smile.

"And you wonder why I didn't want you to meet Adeline and Clover. You guys act like I was such a dick."

None of them say anything. Bryce may have, but she's too busy trying to get Clover to laugh.

This is why he didn't want me to meet

his friends. Because now there's this voice at the back of my mind whispering about whether the Damon Siska I've had for the past seven or so months isn't who he really is. That maybe I've trusted someone who isn't being true to himself. And the only reason that hurts is because I'm already way too invested.

CHAPTER 20
ADELINE

t's been two weeks since I went back to work and one week with our new nanny, Astrid, and I swear I'm about ready to quit my job.

After the longest day ever and the worst drive with the traffic, I park in my new parking spot that Damon is paying for. I was prepared to pay, but he insisted. Since he's the one who asked me to live down here, it was his responsibility. After much arguing, I relented. His Mercedes is parked in the spot beside mine, but that doesn't mean any-thing. Oftentimes he'll catch a ride with Cooper or Miles or hop in an Uber if he doesn't feel like driving.

I don't know why I didn't take him up on getting a driver for me. Yes, I do. Because I know how much it costs. I'm regretting that decision now after dealing with all the idiot drivers on the road today. I swear, put the happiest, most low-key, easygoing person in traffic for a couple of hours, and they'll come out of the car as a vicious, intolerant asshole.

I walk across the street, glancing at Peeper's Alley. I've yet to hang out there, and though I'm looking forward to a night out, tonight I just want to cuddle my baby girl and chill. I walk up the stairs and open the door to the apartment, and the shrill sound of laughter greets me. After slipping off my shoes and hanging my bags on the hooks by the door, I walk in and see no one in the main area.

"You're wet," I hear Damon say, and I stop in my tracks.

"So wet," Astrid says.

My body goes ice cold, and I close my eyes. Please don't tell me he's sleeping with the nanny. My chest gets tight, and my heart rate picks up.

"Feel it, it's soaked," Astrid says.

I can tell now that the voices are coming from Damon's room.

I don't see Clover anywhere, so she must be sleeping in her crib, which is ridiculous. She should not be napping when it's so close to her actual bedtime. I'm trying to get her on a schedule, and I specifically told Astrid that when we hired her.

When we interviewed Astrid, she was so polite, giving me most of her attention. I thought *awesome, she doesn't care about Damon. Maybe she doesn't even follow football.* But that all changed the first day on the job. She laughs at all his jokes—which aren't all that funny—and she paws at him as though they're cats and she's trying to play with him. I've been meaning to mention it to Damon.

But this…

"Ohhh." Astrid again. "Damon!"

Damon laughs. "I gotta get you out of these clothes." God, he's using the same voice he does with Clover.

"Be gentle," Astrid says.

I feel as if I'm in a nightmare.

"I'm always gentle," Damon says.

"With those big hands, you handle something so small perfectly." I can only assume she's talking about her tits. They are small. That's one area I have her beat.

"I'm a master, that's why."

I groan.

"You sure are," Astrid says with a soft purr to her voice that makes bile rise up my throat.

"Shit, Adeline should be home soon. We have to hurry," Damon says.

I step back and sit on the edge of Damon's bed, hearing them scramble.

"But you didn't get everywhere. We have to finish." Again, Astrid uses that stripper voice.

"No, I did. You go ahead and leave. I'll handle the rest myself."

I tilt my head. He's going to jerk off?

"But—" Astrid fights not leaving.

If his hands are on her, I can't blame the girl. I wouldn't want to leave either. I was in her shoes a long time ago.

"I'm good. Plus, your shirt and stuff."

"Yeah, I suppose. Don't want her getting the wrong idea. Okay, I'll see you on Monday. Maybe we can do this again."

"We'll see." Damon's voice has lost some

of the light quality it had earlier. Is he pissed he didn't get to finish with her?

Fucking hell.

The bathroom door opens, and Astrid comes out, her T-shirt soaked through with the outline of her breasts showing. She startles when she sees me. "Adeline!"

"What?" Damon rushes out after her with Clover in a towel, cuddled into his chest. "Hey, Adeline."

It makes me feel a little better about the situation because I know Damon wouldn't be fooling around in front of our daughter. But just a little.

"Guess I missed out on all the action." I meet Damon's gaze.

"I should go." Astrid hurries to the door. "I hope she's not sick. Bye, guys."

I hold Damon's gaze, but as soon as I hear the door to the apartment open and close, I stomp into the kitchen and grab a glass and my bottle of white wine from the fridge.

Damon comes into the kitchen, standing behind the breakfast bar. "You didn't think…"

I pour a heavy amount of white wine into my glass and gulp it down.

"You actually think I'd fuck the nanny?" He laughs, but there's no humor to it.

"Why wouldn't I think that? There are a million romance novels about it. Not to mention, isn't it every guy's wet dream to fuck the hot nanny? It's not out of the realm of possibility." I swallow half the glass.

"Shit, Adeline, Clover had a blowout. I came home, and Astrid was in there trying to clean her up. Didn't know how to use the shower spray properly, and the nozzle went crazy on her. We shut the door a bit so water didn't get everywhere. She soaked her shirt. Go look, you'll see."

He heads into mine and Clover's room—to put her in a diaper and change her, I suppose.

I head into his bathroom and see that it's a disaster. On the floor sits the outfit I put Clover in this morning, covered in poop.

I go back to my room and rest my shoulder on the door frame. "I'm sorry for thinking that. It's just…"

"It's fine. You wouldn't be alone in thinking that. It's who I was, right?"

Was? He's using past tense.

"It has nothing to do with you or your reputation. It's me." I walk away and go to the living room window to look out.

Astrid is waiting at the bus station. Thankfully, she had a sweatshirt she's able to wear even though it's still warm outside.

A couple minutes later, I hear Damon join me in the room. "What do you mean it has to do with you? If I heard the same thing you did, I would've busted in the door. How do women control themselves in those situations? They can wait until nighttime to cut off his dick or plan for months to take his money little by little until they divorce them."

I chuckle. "Haven't you ever heard that revenge is best served cold? While we want revenge, you guys always want to beat up the other guy. In our eyes, you're the one who hurt us, but you guys always blame the other guy. Or maybe hitting him feels good, and you won't hit a woman. I'm not a psychologist." I finish the wine in my glass and go back to the kitchen for more.

Damon puts Clover on the mat that has all the toys hanging down above her and comes over to take the bottle from my hand and pours me a glass. "Talk."

He sits at the breakfast bar across from me and slides the wineglass over to me.

"Astrid is good with Clover, but every time you're here, she's more interested in what you think. She always flirts with you, and I don't like it." I have no idea how I can convey this without outing myself as jealous. "We're doing really well with what we have going, and I don't like how she's trying to come between us. And then with what happened in there, although it was nothing, she looked guilty when she came out of the bathroom."

"Probably because I could practically see her tits. Believe me, I didn't look." He holds up his hands in front of him.

"We're not a couple. You can look. I just don't want someone in this house who wants you or me. I understand there's not a long line of men waiting to nanny our baby and who would want a middle school teacher with a postpartum body, but..." I laugh at my own joke.

Damon doesn't. He just nods, looking more serious than usual. "I understand."

"It's not that I'm jealous," I say, because I want that out there. But I am so jealous, and now I'm sure I'm making it obvious.

He stands and rounds the island. "She's gone. I'll make the call."

"Are you sure you understand…"

He walks into his bedroom while I sulk in the kitchen for another minute.

Eventually, I join Clover on the floor. "I know you might have liked Astrid, but she wasn't here for us, baby. She was just here for Daddy."

———

That night, I lay awake thinking that maybe I had it wrong with Astrid. Is it even feasible to find a nanny who doesn't see Damon as a sex symbol? Maybe it's something I'll just have to get used to.

Clover keeps making noises in her sleep —whimpering or crying for a second or sucking hard on her pacifier. Most nights it doesn't bother me, but tonight I can't block it out and get to sleep. She's been doing excellent at sleeping through the night. We put her down at eleven at night and she sleeps until five or six. So, nighttime feedings aren't much of a thing now.

I throw off the covers, unable to take it anymore. Tomorrow is my day off, and I do not want to spend it asleep on the couch. I tiptoe out of the room, taking the monitor and turning it on once I reach the kitchen. The black leather sofas look so uncomfortable. There's no way I can sleep on those. My eyes shift to the double doors of Damon's bedroom.

No. That's super weird.

Then the doors open, and I step back.

"Adeline?" He squints, his hair mussed. "Fuck, I got up to go to the bathroom and heard someone walking around out here. I thought someone got in or something."

He's in only his boxer briefs, and I try to divert my attention from the outline of his dick. God, he's so gorgeous. *I don't blame you, Astrid. I might've done the same thing.*

"Sorry, she's really restless tonight, and I couldn't sleep. I'm just going to take the sofa."

He steps back and motions into his room. "Get in my bed, Adeline." His voice is deep and husky from just waking up, and my libido perks up and takes notice.

"Oh no." I shake my head.

"It's a king. I won't even know you're there… unless you want me to."

I swallow hard. There's been no conversation about anything sex-related since the night I delivered. It's as though we're both pretending it never happened.

"Are you sure?" I lift the monitor. "I have this in case she wakes up."

"Just get in and let's sleep."

He walks into his room, then goes into the bathroom. I'm still standing outside of the room when he comes back out.

"Stop thinking so much. We're friends. And it's not like you haven't slept there before." He laughs at his own joke but sobers a bit when I still haven't moved. "If you don't get in this bed, I'm going to pick you up and drop you on it. Sound familiar?" He arches an eyebrow.

He remembers that night? How? He must have had hundreds just like it.

I nod. "Okay, just tonight."

"And Sunday," he says.

I frown. "Sunday?"

"I'll be out of town."

"Oh right."

Anyone in my head right now would think I get off on torturing myself. I slide under his sheet and comforter, instantly cocooned in the musky scent of his body wash. I might never leave.

"Good night," he whispers into the dark.

"Good night, Damon."

His breathing evens out after a few minutes while I remain wide awake. I'm in Damon Siska's bed again. But if someone had told me the first time I was here that I'd be back under these circumstances, feeling this way about the man sleeping beside me, I would've said they were crazy.

CHAPTER 21
DAMON

I would never tell Adeline now because there's no point and it would just upset her, but Astrid did make her interest in me obvious more than once after she found out from Adeline that we aren't a couple. And while I was trying to bathe Clover, she was pushing her wet tits on my arm. If Adeline hadn't broached the subject, I would have that night anyway. I want someone here only for Clover.

Because of the short notice, we had to use Adeline's mom for a week again. Clover went back and forth every day, with Adeline's mom picking her up at the middle school when Adeline got there.

We had another away game and Adeline slept in my bed again, and now my sheets all smell like her. She must have moved to my side last night because her scent is on my pillow. I told her she could sleep in my bed every night, but she got earplugs instead. What was I going to say? *I want you to sleep with me. I like having your body next to mine. It's comforting except for the part where it's a major cock tease.*

Fuck, my dick is eventually going to screw up this situation for me, I just know it.

I'm not a relationship kind of guy. What happened with Greta made me swear off them, and that will never change. I'll never put myself in that position again, no matter how much I want the woman.

When morning arrives, I've barely had any sleep. I have to go in and watch film, so I climb out of my warm bed to shower.

Hearing Adeline and Clover already up, I peek my head out of my bedroom first. "New nanny should be here within a half hour."

"I still don't know how I feel about you picking someone on your own," Adeline says.

Adeline was in the classroom when the interviews had to be done by phone, so I took the lead on this one.

"We didn't have a lot of choices. I picked the best candidate of all the ones I talked to."

"Oh, I see how this goes." She must've had a rough night too, but she'll be happy when she sees who I hired because there will be no need to worry about who the nanny is here for.

I shower, dress to go in, and pack my bag, placing it by the door before going to the kitchen to fix myself breakfast.

"How's my girl this morning?" I bend down and kiss Clover, who is sitting on Adeline's lap, and now my head is dangerously close to Adeline's breast. It's covered, but damn, it's pillowy soft, and I just wish I could burrow my face in there.

"She's not taking her bottle well, and I swear she still seems hungry after she finishes. I think this weekend we might have to start introducing baby food. Remember Dr. Gregory brought it up last time?"

Vaguely. I'm usually really attentive at our pediatrician visits, but Dr. Gregory was the fill-in for our actual pediatrician, Dr. Bennett. And Dr. Gregory seemed more into Adeline than Clover. He got a little too excited when Adeline told him we're coparents, not a couple. I don't see why we have to tell people that anyway. It's none of their business. I didn't tell the new nanny, and I don't plan to.

The doorbell rings, so I go open the door.

"Glad you were able to make it," I say, shaking the nanny's hand.

"Same. I'm Haze."

"Good to know. Let me introduce you to Adeline and Clover." I walk him into the family room.

Adeline stares at us, still trying to get Clover interested in her bottle.

"Adeline, this is Haze, our new nanny." I clap him on the back, and he tilts forward slightly. Note to self: do not do that again.

"Oh, hi." She stands and puts out her hand.

They shake hands.

"You're lucky I just finished another job. All the kids are in school now. I was with them for eight years." The guy looks as though he might cry over it. "May I?" Haze asks, nodding toward Clover. Adeline prepares to hand her over, but Haze stops her. "I almost forgot. Let me get all the city germs off of me."

He walks into the kitchen area and washes his hands. Adeline smiles as if she likes that he's so good with that stuff. Whatever. He washed his hands, not solved world famine.

When he returns, he sits on the leather sofa and cradles Clover in his arms, teasing her lips with the bottle. Adeline and I stare at him from behind the couch.

"Sometimes I play a game," Haze tells us. "And Adeline, a little history about me since we're just talking for the first time... I worked with a family on the Northshore for eight years. Saw three of their kids, from newborn to the last one, who just went to kindergarten this year, which is why I'm available for you guys. I was told that your identities would be kept confidential until I arrived, so I assume one of you must be in the public eye. Which one of you is it?"

Adeline makes a sound, then purses her lips to hold in her laugh.

"I already signed the NDA you sent to the office, plus I would never," Haze says.

"It's Damon!" Adeline says. "He's the wide receiver for the Chicago Grizzlies." She hits me in the arm and points at Haze because the fucker got Clover to take the bottle.

I have to remind myself that it's his job. I can't be jealous. It's his first damn day.

"I don't follow football. Sorry, Damon, no offense." He cringes a little.

I shrug. "None taken."

"And what about you, Adeline?" Haze looks up at her expectantly.

She rounds the back of the couch and sits on the chair, crossing her legs. She's wearing a dress today, and her bare legs look silky smooth. "I teach middle school."

"Oh, a much more honorable career."

I roll my eyes and go to the kitchen to make my breakfast while Adeline thinks it's comedy hour, barely holding in her laughter.

"No offense, Damon, it just seems like football is all 'I hit you, you hit me,'" Haze calls.

That actually does piss me off. I pop my head out of the kitchen. "Maybe you can come down to the stadium sometime. I'll have Cooper Rice throw you a ball and can dodge Miles Cavanaugh to try to catch it."

Adeline loses the battle with her laughter and fails to recover many times over. It's actually cute, but I'm not telling her that.

"I assume those are other players?" Haze whispers to Adeline.

She nods. "They live in the building too."

"Adeline," I snipe.

"He signed an NDA," she says to me over her shoulder.

"Okay, so I'm usually home around five thirty. You never know with Damon. Sometimes he beats me home. Everything in her room is pretty much where you'd expect. She's on formula, and I wrote down the amounts over by the bottles. I left both of our cell phone numbers, as well as my mom's, in case you can't get a hold of either of us. The stroller and carrier are by the front door. There's a park not too far away."

"Maybe just stay in today," I say.

"Actually, there's a group I host that I would love to take Clover to for a little interaction," Haze says.

I narrow my eyes. "She's five months old. What interaction does she need?"

"Oh, it's for the adults."

Clover fidgets in his arms.

"Yeah, no." I hope he can tell I'm not joking.

"Maybe if you give us more specifics, Damon and I can discuss it later, Haze." She looks at him sweetly. "I gotta go before I'm late." She stands and goes over to give Clover a kiss goodbye.

Haze raises one hand. "She's feeding so well. She knows you love her."

"What?" I step out of the kitchen.

Adeline straightens and walks over to me, putting her hand on my chest. "It's fine. Honestly. Have a great day." She rises on her toes and is about to kiss me on the lips, but she freezes, and we lock eyes. "Shoot, sorry. Not sure where that came from."

She grabs her bags and walks out the door with another goodbye, leaving me standing there wondering what that was and why it didn't feel weird to me.

I should go too. I finish eating my breakfast in the kitchen, listening to Haze talk to Clover about all the adventures they're going to have and how he's so happy to be her host. What the hell?

When there's a knock on the door, I assume it's Miles since we're driving in together. I open the door and grab my bag. Of course, Miles can't stay outside. He has to come on in.

"Shit, this place is crazy different. Where are all the G-strings and bowls of condoms?" Miles stops when he sees Haze with Clover on the couch. His head whips in my direction, clearly questioning who he is.

"Miles Cavanaugh, meet Haze, our new nanny. And no worries, he doesn't know who you are."

Miles offers his hand, but Haze scrunches up his nose, shaking his head. "Germs and babies don't mix."

Miles nods. "Good to meet you. Let's go." He heads out the door.

I say goodbye to Haze, then my baby girl. I don't care if he doesn't like it.

Once we're walking down the stairs, we knock on Cooper's door. He screams that he'll be right out.

"A male nanny, huh? I'm surprised," Miles says.

"The other one hit on me, but we're not telling Adeline that. Plus, she wasn't respecting Adeline's place in our family, so we got rid of her. This is good, because Haze's attention will be on Clover only."

"Why do you say that?" Miles's head tilts to the side.

Cooper's door opens, and he files out with Ellery right behind him. We both raise our eyebrows because she obviously spent the night.

"I fell asleep watching a movie. I'm late. See you guys." She kisses Cooper's cheek, runs down the stairs, and hops on her bike, heading in the direction of the hospital.

"What's up?" Cooper says, seeming his usual self. I swear I don't get those two.

Miles thumbs in my direction. "Siska got a male nanny."

"A manny?" Cooper laughs.

I shrug and start down the stairs. "I guess."

"But he thinks this solves the problem of their caretaker being attracted to one of them and not putting Clover's needs first. Do you agree, Cooper?"

Miles really pisses me off sometimes, and he's succeeding right now.

"Is Haze gay?" Cooper asks.

Miles's eyes widen.

"I don't know. That has nothing to do with whether he's qualified or not," I say.

"Agreed. But you never thought that maybe a male nanny might be into Adeline? You do realize the woman who had your baby is hot, right?" Cooper asks. "There're a lot of guys who would give their right nut to be with her."

Does he think I'm blind? I see the looks she gets when we're out together. Though the majority of them are from me lately because I'm constantly undressing her in my mind.

"And if Haze was gay, he could still be into you," Miles says.

"I hate you both." I walk out of the building and cross the street as their laughter rings out behind me.

"Well, you better be prepared for her to get some male attention because Bryce is taking her out Saturday night. And no worries about that ticket to our games. I did some digging and got the seat next to Bryce and Ellery for Adeline for the rest of the season."

"Shit, Cavanaugh, I was going to do it, but I wanted to make sure she even wanted to go."

"Sorry, Bryce wanted her there, and it's my job to give my fiancée what she wants."

"Remind me not to get whipped like you two," Cooper says, nodding at someone we pass who gives us a double-take, obviously recognizing us.

I press the button on my fob to unlock my Mercedes. "You're already whipped, you're just not getting the pussy."

Miles laughs. "Neither are you, Siska. I'm the only one getting laid on the regular. No wonder you're both grumpy pricks."

"Fuck you," Cooper and I say at the same time.

I start my SUV and pull out of the parking garage. Hell, I was thinking that Adeline would feel more comfortable with a male nanny, but I can't have him flirting with her. There's no fucking way I'll be able to tolerate that, which means at this point, who will we find to be our nanny?

The line between us is blurring more and more every fucking day.

CHAPTER 22
ADELINE

"I don't know about this," I say in the bedroom. "Nothing fits right."

"Let me see," Damon calls out from the other side of the door.

"How can my boobs still be bigger when I stopped breastfeeding?"

"Stop it and get your ass out here."

I open the door, thinking about calling Bryce and telling her there's no way I can go on this girls' night out. I have a muffin top over my pants, and no jacket is going to hide it.

Damon has Clover in her bouncy seat and is feeding her the baby food we've started introducing to her. She's just like her daddy, not very picky, which has worked out well for us. The spoon hovers near Clover's mouth as Damon's gaze tracks down my body. It's a sexy as hell look, as though he'd like to take me to his room and strip these clothes off of me.

Clover whines, and he blinks, turning his attention back to her.

"You look fine. I don't see the problem," he says.

I walk over to the full-length mirror near the entry that allows me to see my whole outfit. "I'm not going for *fine*. And I'm probably going to be hot in these pants."

I fiddle with the black pants. My blouse is tight, off the shoulders, and dips at my cleavage. My makeup looks good though, which is surprising. After all these months of not really doing much with it, I was still able to accomplish the look I wanted.

Looking at my reflection, I spy Damon behind me, his eyes meeting mine. Okay, no need to be self-conscious, he obviously likes what he sees. Why does that make my stomach feel funny?

There's a knock on the door, and Bryce shouts to Damon to release me, which makes me laugh and Damon grumble. I open the door, sliding into my heels, finishing off the outfit.

"Whoa, mama, you are smokin'." Bryce walks into the apartment. "Isn't she, Damon?"

"He said I look *fine*," I say.

She rolls her eyes behind his back, then sits on the stool next to him. "Hi, Clover. You've got Daddy all to yourself tonight."

Bryce is wearing a dress, and I wonder if I should've done the same. Chicago weather is a little cooler at night this time of year, but still, it can be warm if where we're going is busy, and I don't want to be sweating all night.

"I'm her favorite man," Damon says in that cocky way that seems to come naturally to him.

"What about Haze?" she asks, and I bite my lip to stop from laughing.

Damon shoots her a death glare, and Bryce laughs.

Haze is great. Definitely made to be a

nanny, but he and Damon aren't seeing eye to eye on a lot of things. One being Damon wants to put an ankle bracelet on him so he stays within a two-block radius. I honestly think Damon just doesn't like sharing Clover's attention with another man.

Watching Bryce and Damon interact is comical and what I needed after a long week.

"Have fun, Clover and Daddy. I'm sure Miles and Cooper will be over soon. And don't worry, I'll have her back before you leave for the game in the morning."

"What?" Damon asks, spinning around in his seat to look at me.

Bryce laughs. "Huh, I think someone might be scared he's gonna be replaced." She raises her eyebrows.

I walk over to Damon and kiss Clover's cheek. "Good night, baby girl. Be good for Daddy." I turn to Damon, and his eyes are on my cleavage. "If you need me to come home early, just call me."

"Nope. No way," Bryce says. "There will be three men here. Surely they can handle a baby. Rent that old movie about that if you need tips." She tugs on my sleeve. "Let's go. Quick getaway."

"Have fun, you deserve it." Damon wipes Clover's mouth and picks her up out of her seat, walking us to the door.

I look at them again, finding it hard to leave. Bryce clears her throat behind me.

"Okay, bye," I say.

"Bye, Mommy." Damon lifts Clover's hand and waves it.

I nod. "Bye."

I circle around to Bryce before I shove her out the door and lock it so I can stay. I'm a mom, a working mom, so the guilt of leaving her when it's my free time is almost unbearable as we walk down the stairs.

"This is good for Damon. He needs to see you going out and not waiting around for him." She pulls out her phone. "Here's our car. We're meeting Elle there."

"I'm not waiting around for him," I say, sliding into the back seat after her.

"Sure, you aren't."

The driver verifies with Bryce where we're going, and I drop the subject of Damon because I don't really want to think about him tonight. He's constantly in my head anyway. I could use a little break.

When we enter the restaurant, Ellery's hand is waving in the air at a table in the back. She's already got some type of cocktail with fruit in it on the table in front of her.

"Hey, ladies." She slides out of her chair and hugs us. "Tell me Damon's tongue was on the floor when you left?" She and Bryce share a conspiratorial grin.

"Sure as hell was," Bryce says, laughing.

"I'm not sure about that. I think he was just surprised," I say. "He's literally never seen me dressed like this. Even when we hooked up, I was in ball game clothes."

"Yes, can we talk about that night?" Ellery asks. "As a doctor, I'm wondering how our little Clover came into being with so many birth control options out there."

"Elle!" Bryce scolds.

Thankfully, the waitress comes over. We both order some rum drink they have on special.

"I'm sorry, Bryce is right. It's none of my business." Ellery sips her drink, shaking her head. I have a feeling Ellery may have already finished off another drink before we arrived.

"It's fine. Honestly, I don't really know. I don't like being on birth control if I'm not in a relationship—it gives me too many side effects—so I wasn't on it at the time. We used condoms, but nothing is a hundred percent, so…" I shrug.

Ellery and Bryce look at one another, sharing a similar expression, and I can tell they're about to bring up his reputation once again. I don't know any of them very well, but I'm kind of sick of the jokes at Damon's expense.

"Listen, I know Damon's no saint, but he really has only treated me with respect. I realize you both know a very different version of him, but he's been good to Clover and me." This is not how I wanted girls' night to start out, but I can't sit here all night and have them put him down when he's done nothing but try to lift me up since he found out I was pregnant. He could very well be the one out tonight and me home with Clover.

Bryce reacts first, her hand flying over mine and squeezing. "I'm sorry. You're right. We won't start in with any jokes, and we won't disrespect what you two have." She looks at Ellery and back at me. "We're honestly surprised the two of you haven't gotten together as a couple. But I know I make fun of Damon a lot, and I'll stop. You're right, being a dad has changed him."

"Thanks, and as far as if we're going to be together or not, the answer is no. We don't want to jeopardize the easy relationship we have going on right now. Clover has to come first." Thank goodness the waitress comes and drops our drinks. I take a quick sip to cool myself down.

"Eventually that's going to change though, right?" Bryce asks. She's definitely the bolder one of the two. "I mean, are the two of you going to stay together and celibate until Clover's eighteen?"

I laugh, not even able to imagine that. The last five months since Damon gave me an orgasm have been torture. "That's a hard no."

"At some point, one of you will find someone else, and things will change. I mean, could you be in the room next door, hearing Damon banging someone else?" Bryce asks.

"I think we shouldn't talk about Damon for the rest of the night. It's supposed to be girls' night out." Ellery is quick to chime in.

I appreciate what Bryce is saying. She's making me see it from an outsider's perspective, staring into the perfect little snow globe of a life that Damon and I have created. It's what friends should do, but tonight I just want to have a few drinks and not think too far into the future.

"Elle is right. Forget it. I really like you, and—"

"Don't worry, she was as blind as you before she got with Miles." Ellery laughs, stopping the waitress and asking for a round of tequila shots. "We're going to restart this girls' night."

Things improve from there, and we all talk about our different jobs. Ellery's is probably the most interesting—she seems to come across all kinds of people at the hospital. The only stories I can tell are about prepubescent boys and girls, but some of them are good for a laugh, too.

About an hour later, Ellery leans over the

table toward me. "There's a guy checking you out."

Bryce looks in the direction Ellery indicates and nods. "He's hot too."

"Oh, I'm not looking to hook up or anything," I say, but Ellery waves him over. "Ellery!"

"This is girls' night out," Bryce says with a bit of a whine in her voice.

"I know, but it's also Adeline's first night out since she had Clover." Then Ellery looks at me. "I'm not suggesting you go to the bathroom and screw his brains out, but a little interest from a guy never hurts the ego." She shrugs.

"Hey," a deep voice says from behind me.

"Hi." I turn, and he sidles up to me, way too close for comfort.

"Hi. I'm Ellery." She sticks her hand out over the table to him. "This is Bryce, and this is Adeline." She finishes with her hands directed at me as though I'm center stage.

He nods. "Lincoln. Good to meet you all."

Lincoln asks the table next to us if they're using the empty chair and slides it over to join us. He's attractive, to be sure, but the opposite of Damon. The tattoos up and down his arms say he has an edge that implies he's rebellious in ways Damon isn't.

Oh my god, brain, stop comparing him to Damon.

"Can I buy you a drink, Adeline?" he asks. "All of you, actually."

Ellery smiles. "Sure."

I glance at Ellery, but she turns and starts a conversation with Bryce about someone they went to college together with, leaving me no choice but to talk to Lincoln. I find out he owns his own tattoo parlor in the city and doesn't live far from the bar we're at. He moved to Chicago ten years ago from Milwaukee, and he loves it. He tells me about his favorite restaurants and how there's one specifically he'd love to take me to.

Panic ensues.

"I have a baby," I blurt.

Bryce almost spits out her drink while Ellery laughs.

"Oh yeah?" Lincoln chuckles as though he's not sure what to make of that.

Seriously, Adeline, you can't get through one

conversation with a hot guy without telling him you have a baby?

"Yeah, she's five months old and with her dad today."

He nods. I can tell I've probably lost his interest, but I've never been in this situation. I don't know what to do. And besides, I'm not interested anyway.

He asks me her name and eventually excuses himself, saying he sees someone he knows.

I down the rest of my drink in one gulp.

"Okay, so we have to start from scratch. You're a little rusty." Bryce smiles.

"Yeah, he doesn't get your life story for just one drink." Ellery laughs again. "I'm so happy I was here when that happened though. It was the funniest thing I've seen all week."

"Happy to be the entertainment." I shake my head and laugh at myself.

We have another drink, and I'm feeling slightly buzzed when we return to "The Den." Both Bryce and I are struggling a little up the stairs—whether because of our heels or the drinks, I'm not sure.

"I tried to get Miles to install an elevator.

Maybe you can ask Damon. He's Daddy Warbucks." Bryce heaves for breath by the time we get to Damon's place.

"I can ask, but I'm only here until the season is over." I chuckle.

She stops, looking surprised. "What?"

I nod. "Damon asked me to move in here so he wouldn't have to commute during the season, then he'll move out by me for the offseason."

"Oh, I didn't know that." She hugs me. "I'm going to go screw my fiancé, and hopefully they'll win because of it tomorrow. I'll come and grab you before the game. Text you in the morning with a time."

"Sounds good. Thanks for taking me out."

"Oh, you don't have to thank me. We're going to be great friends."

The door opens behind me, startling me. Damon stands there in a pair of athletic shorts and no shirt, the tattoos on his arms and chest on display.

God damn, the alcohol has further weakened my willpower because the buzzing between my legs right now is more demanding than usual.

"Afraid someone walked her home?" Bryce cackles, walking up the stairs.

"Your loud-ass mouth woke me up," Damon calls back.

I step in, slipping off my heels. "God, I haven't worn shoes like that in so long, my feet are killing me." I grab a ponytail holder off the counter and secure my hair back. I'd undo my pants if he wasn't standing here looking at me.

My gaze meets his, and I find it lust-filled and heady.

My nipples pebble in my bra. "What?"

"You're so fucking sexy."

I blink a few times. "I'm sorry?"

He walks toward me until our chests brush. "You heard me."

I place my hand on his chest. "I heard it, but I don't understand what's happening here."

"How much have you had to drink tonight?"

"Just a couple drinks. I'm fine, a little buzzed, but fine. What's going on?"

"Adeline." He slides his hand along my cheek, and I can't help how my eyes drift closed for a moment. "It's been months since

I've had sex, and I'm going to be real fucking honest here, I'm dying. And seeing you tonight..." He runs his thumb along my bottom lip, and his eyes drop to my cleavage. "These tits." His tongue slides along his bottom lip. "It's all I could think of when you were gone. All night, I've been imagining what I would do to you if I got you naked and in my bed."

Oh shit. I am so turned on right now, but some part of my non-lizard brain must be working because I say, "But it might ruin what we have." My hands run down his muscled chest, dipping in the valleys of his lower abdomen in what has to be the pinnacle of mixed messages.

He bites his lower lip before he speaks again. "The way I see it, we can have the best of both worlds. I need to have sex, and I'm pretty sure you need it too." His other hand wraps around my waist, tugging me harder against him. "I need to fuck you. You've made me a desperate man."

I need to fuck him too.

"Okay, just this once."

I barely get the words out before Damon smashes his lips to mine. Months of pent-up lust explodes between us—our hands are frantic and groping, our lips devouring, our chests heaving.

This is going to come back and bite me. I know it. But right now, I don't care, especially when his hard length presses into my stomach. All I want is for that to be inside me when I come apart.

I climb him like a tree. "Take me to your room."

CHAPTER 23
ADELINE

"This is such a bad idea," I murmur once we're inside the bedroom, more to myself than for him.

Damon's hand runs down my throat, and my head falls back, his lips casting open-mouth kisses along my heated flesh.

"No, this is the best thing we've ever done." He brings my head up and locks eyes with me as if he's sealing a promise. "Except Clover. She'll always be the best."

"She's perfect," I whisper.

"She's beautiful like her mommy." His thumb runs down my throat. "So fucking beautiful."

I clench my thighs together, not from his

words but from his eyes, the way he looks at me. Then I press my lips to his, and my moan spills into his mouth. His fingers tighten their hold on the threads of my hair before he strips his lips from mine.

"My dick was hard all night thinking about you in that outfit. Your ass." He reaches down with his free hand and slaps my left ass cheek. "And Jesus, these tits." The same hand grazes up my body and molds to my breast, pushing down the fabric of my blouse until his thumb runs over my nipple. "Tell me to stop because I'm about to snap."

I do exactly the opposite.

"Fuck me, Damon," I rasp, barely able to breathe from the adrenaline pulsing through my veins.

He thrusts his tongue into my mouth until our tongues tangle in a dance that feels natural. I wait for him to strip his lips from mine, say something dirty, but instead he takes his time with the kiss, and I sink into him. My core clenches with every stroke of his tongue, remembering the feeling of it between my legs. My fingers entwine in his short hair, wishing he had more for me to pull on.

He shifts us, his hand running down the valley of my breasts to the button of my pants. With one hand, he flicks open the button, and I groan, desperate for him to feel how wet I am. My zipper slides down, and he slips two fingers under the top of my panties, moving his fingers back and forth.

"How wet are you?"

I smile at him. "Why don't you find out for yourself?"

Instead of dipping his hand lower, he steps back, and I feel cold and empty without his hands and lips on me. "Take them off for me."

He crosses his arms over his impressive, bare chest, his hard dick tenting his shorts.

I hook my fingers on either side of my pants and shimmy them down my legs.

"Did you shave for some asshole tonight?"

"No."

"Good." He squeezes his dick through his shorts. "The blouse too."

I lower the zipper on the side and peel it off my body, leaving me in only a black thong since I wasn't wearing a bra with this shirt.

He strips out of his shorts, taking his long, thick length and pumping it with his hand. "I deserve a fucking medal for staying away as long as I have."

God, I don't remember Damon being so lustful over my body before, and it boosts my ego since he's seen me pre-baby, extremely pregnant, and now postpartum.

"Why are you still over there?" I climb back onto his bed, kneeling near the edge.

He watches me for another second before approaching me, his hand slowly stroking himself. As soon as he's close enough, I cast small kisses along his chest, my hands running up and down and around to his back, then down to his firm ass. I squeeze it, and he growls.

His hand dips under the elastic of my thong, running over the length of my pussy and finding me soaking wet. "Fuuuuck." He thrusts a finger inside me.

I tip my head back and moan, staring up at him with my mouth open because it feels so good. He gently massages my clit with his thumb, and oh my god, it's been too long. I'm practically ready to come apart already.

Damon must see the pleading in my eyes because he smirks, knowing he has me right where he wants me. He pushes another finger inside me, and the lazy circles on my clit make me fall forward, forehead on his chest. I suck on his nipple, needing something to distract me from the orgasm trying to rush through me.

"Go ahead, there's plenty more to come," he whispers, and I lay my cheek on his chest, staring up at him as I fall apart on his fingers.

Once I've come down a little, he presses his mouth to mine, possessive and frantic. He lowers me to the mattress, using his strong thighs to open my legs as my back falls into the plushness of his mattress.

"I promise, after this first time, I'll make it last longer and give you so many more."

I giggle as he reaches over to his drawer and pulls out a condom. I hold his hand as he rises on his knees to put it on. "Should we check it or something?"

He places it at my mouth. "Bite it." I put

my teeth on the package, and he tears it open. "We couldn't be that lucky twice."

"Ha, says the man who wasn't pregnant."

He takes out the condom and rolls it down his length.

"I didn't even get to taste you." I stick out my bottom lip in a pout.

"We're not done. I just need to come to calm myself the fuck down. And then we'll have all kinds of time to play." He stares between my legs, his teeth biting into his lower lip. "Show me."

His large hand runs down my inner thigh, and goosebumps follow his path. Slowly, I open my legs, feeling a little shy about it because this is the first time a man is seeing me since I gave birth. But as usual, Damon doesn't make me feel self-conscious at all.

With a growl in the back of his throat, he falls on top of me, his tip pushing against my opening. My hands cling to his shoulders, and he sinks inside me inch by inch until he's fully seated and stretching me in the best way.

"Oh my god," I say, pressing my head back into the mattress.

He moves inside me, slowly at first, but the more the sounds of how wet I am echo through the quiet bedroom, his pace increases until he's fucking me so hard and so fast you'd think we were being timed to win a race.

I wrap my legs around his middle, and he sets one leg on his shoulder, driving into me so deeply I cry out, only to cover my mouth. Clover cannot wake up right now.

"Adeline, you're gonna be the death of me." He inches down and takes my nipple into his mouth, teasing the hard nub with his tongue.

My hands tug and pull, scratching his back as though I want to consume him. He shifts his attention to my other nipple, and my back arches off the mattress.

"God, yes." The pull between my legs becomes more insistent.

His teeth nibble, and for the second time within minutes, my body is pulsing with the need to come. He stares at me through those dark eyelashes, a smile toying at his lips, and he opens his mouth so I can see him bite my nipple. After all this time, they're still so sensitive, and my entire body tenses as wave after wave of pure ecstasy crashes through me.

He doesn't stop or slow down. His mouth pops off my breast, meeting my mouth with the hunger of a starved man as he drives into me over and over. Just when he must be getting close, he tears his mouth from mine, resting his face by my ear. He speaks so quietly that I can't catch what he's saying, only the desperate tone of it, but it's hot as hell witnessing him lose control.

Damon buries his head into the crook of my neck. "Fucking hell."

His hips buck once, then twice before he stills. He falls on me, and we lie there trying to catch our breaths.

Of course, Damon is still the best sex I've ever had.

"I'll be right back," he says and pulls out of me, rolling over to dispose of the condom in the bathroom.

I already feel empty without him. This is not good.

———

I wake up alone in Damon's bed with Clover screaming in my ear. With my face still buried in the pillow, I reach out, and the monitor falls to the floor. Awesome.

I toss the covers off me, and the cooler air that meets me reminds me of last night.

I'm completely naked.

As I'm mentally going back over last night, the bathroom door opens, and Damon emerges with just a towel on.

"I'll get her." He winks.

Seeing him undressed has me thinking again about last night, when we had sex not once but twice. I got hungry and was in the kitchen eating a piece of cold pizza when he pushed me onto the breakfast bar, spread me open, and told me he was only hungry for one thing. That escalated, and soon I was riding him on the kitchen chair.

As if I need proof, I look around the room to find our clothes are discarded all over the floor.

I take the sheet off his bed, wrap it around myself, and go into my bedroom. He's changing Clover out of her nighttime onesie.

"Don't be shy on my account," he says, checking me out from the corner of his eye.

A strangled noise squeaks out of me, and I grab a pair of pajamas, which I quickly put on.

"Do you mind doing her bottle and stuff? I have to get ready to go to the stadium," he says.

If I was worried about keeping him up too late, I needn't have bothered. He seems chipper and wide awake this morning.

"Sure, I'll do it." He hands her to me, and I kiss Clover's cheeks. "Did you have fun with Daddy last night?"

"Not as much fun as her mommy had." He laughs and walks out of the room.

"Damon!" I follow him right into his bathroom, where he's putting on deodorant. As he styles his hair, I sit on the toilet with Clover in my arms.

"Stop overthinking it, Adeline. I can hear your thoughts from here." He doesn't move his gaze away from what he's doing in the mirror.

"I just need to make sure we're on the same page."

He taps Clover's nose and pulls back,

then moves forward, and she thinks it's the funniest thing ever.

"Can we focus?" I ask.

He sighs. "I'm not going to have sex with anyone else if that's what you're concerned about."

He walks back out into the bedroom.

I groan and follow, going to sit on the edge of his bed. "Does it change things for us?"

He drops the towel and pulls on his boxers, no shame at all. I guess since I came all over said dick twice last night, what would be the point of being shy about it?

"No. We talked about it last night. We're in this weird situation. We're both horny as hell, so we might as well reap the benefits." He shrugs as though it's no big deal.

To him, maybe it isn't. But I worry that my feelings are going to get entangled, not just my libido.

At the same time, what he's saying kind of makes sense. When that guy hit on me last night, the idea of going back to his place to hook up didn't sound appealing. At all. Then I came home and saw a shirtless Damon, and my libido revved right up. God help me.

"So, it was a one-time thing?" I just need to put boundaries on this whole thing in my mind.

"Do you want it to be a one-time thing?" he asks.

I glance over and see him buttoning up his dress shirt. Oh crap, he's going to put on a suit. I might as well just find my vibrator right now.

"Well… last night was nice." There, that sounded sort of noncommittal, right?

He pins me with a heated stare. "It was fucking hot, and I'm gonna be honest, I don't think I'm done."

I nod. "So, it's roommates-slash-co-parents with benefits then?"

He comes over, his slacks open, his shirt-tails out, and squats in front of Clover and me. "You can call it whatever you want, but it's us fucking."

"Okay." I've never had ongoing sex with someone without commitment before, but I can do it. I *want* to do it. I just don't want to be hurt in the end. But the idea of Damon doing it with someone else… that hurts more.

He stands, tucks in his shirt, and does up his pants and belt. "I'll see you at the game. Your mom coming to watch Clover?" He walks by me, kissing Clover's hand quickly when she reaches for him. "Daddy has to go to work." He grabs his suit jacket. "Clover, tell Mommy to get her tongue back in her mouth. Daddy gets penalized if he's late."

I pick up a pillow and throw it at him. "Shut up."

He laughs, catching it and tossing it back on the bed.

"I hope those hands are just as good in today's game."

He raises his eyebrows at me and sets his suit jacket on the dresser, then rushes over and tickles me in the ribcage.

"Hey, I have your daughter here."

"Just wait, the first touchdown is for you." He winks, picks up his suit jacket, and kisses Clover on her cheek, then me on the lips. "To be continued," he whispers, and my core clenches.

I follow him into the living area when

the doorbell rings. Damon opens it before grabbing his game bag.

Miles stands in the archway but doesn't come in. "Hey, Adeline." He lifts his hand and says in a baby voice, "Hi, Clover."

"Hey, Miles."

"Bryce has your ticket. See you there."

"Have a great game, guys. Tell Cooper for me too."

"Thanks," they say in unison.

As soon as the door shuts behind them, I lift Clover into the air. "Oh, Mommy is a goner for your daddy."

She smiles and makes a noise that sounds suspiciously like, "Duh."

CHAPTER 24

DAMON

"You fucked her!" Cooper says a little too loudly for my liking.

I'm not a kiss-and-tell kind of guy, but Miles kept going on and on about how flushed Adeline's cheeks were this morning. He said he knew something happened and would not let it go. When he asked if we had sex, I felt like I couldn't lie. He's my best friend, and I trust him.

"We're in a mutually beneficial situation, which leaves you, Cooper, on an island by yourself." I clap him on the back.

"Your island is going to implode and sink into the ocean." He closes his eyes, stretching since we're about to be called out to start the game.

"You have no idea what you're talking about. I have the best of both worlds."

Cooper and Miles exchange a look as if I'm some dumbass, but they don't know Adeline and me. How good we are together. This co-parenting thing would have been a nightmare with anyone else.

Cooper pats me on the back and lowers his voice. "You're fucking your daughter's mother, and you're not even in a relationship. Give me one way where this turns out for the better?"

I crack my neck and jump up and down. Maybe he's got a point.

No, we know what we're doing.

They tell us it's time to charge out to the field. I run, and when I get to the sidelines, I search out Adeline. Sure enough, she's there with Bryce and Ellery. She's got my number, twenty-three, written on her cheek, and she's wearing a Grizzlies sweatshirt. She smiles and gives me a small wave.

Yeah, Cooper and Miles don't know what the hell they're talking about. We can so handle this.

"Siska!" Coach calls, and I run over. "Get your eyes off the damn stands and on this game."

"Yes, sir." I nod.

By the half, we're up on the Vipers by one touchdown. Of course, I haven't gotten a touchdown myself because the assholes are double-teaming me on purpose. I'm going to make a touchdown this game, no matter what.

Coop is drinking water on the bench when I sit down next to him. Bryce is screaming for Miles since he's on the field.

"Seriously, she doesn't even need a microphone," I say.

Cooper laughs. "She loves her man."

Those two got engaged so quickly, I don't understand it. I push that thought aside. "I need a touchdown."

Cooper looks over his shoulder and waves to Ellery. "For Adeline?"

"No."

He cocks an eyebrow.

"Fine, yes."

"Talk to Coach." He nods in Coach's direction.

"You heard him at halftime. Everything

is going Bradley's way because they're double-teaming me. I can get open. Pass me the ball."

He blows out a breath. I love Cooper, and he's a great quarterback, but he's a rule-follower. But he's also one of my closest friends.

"I swear to God, Damon, if you don't catch the ball and run it in for a touchdown, I'm gonna make you eat the pigskin."

I hold up my hands. "Deal."

He shakes his head. "You do understand that you don't have to impress her, right? She knows you're a good player. This feels a little high-schoolish." He stands and pulls on his helmet since the offense is going back out there.

"Hey, maybe if you tried to impress Ellery a little more, she'd be more than just your best friend." I pat his back and run out onto the field.

"Asshole!" he shouts from behind me.

I raise my hands as I run out there to get the crowd going. I need their energy because my ego might have bit off more than it can chew with this play. Especially if I'm going to have two guys on me.

We get into the huddle, Cooper glaring at me from the corner of his eye. "Listen, guys, Siska wants a touchdown. Coach wants me to throw to Bradley. We're going to Siska. I'm faking it to Bradley with the hopes their defense goes that way, but we're going to Siska."

"I'll get a jump on them," I say.

He points at me. "Let's hope so. If I get my ass reamed for calling an audible, I'm gonna strangle you."

We all line up, Cooper calls for the ball from the center, and I fucking run, faking out the cornerback, leaving me and the safety to fight it out.

"Not today," I say and act as if I'm going right, but shift left.

Because of Cooper Rice's brilliant arm, as soon as I'm open, the ball sails right into my hands. I run it in for a touchdown.

The crowd roars, and the Jumbotron lights up. Cooper runs up to me, smacking me on the helmet, and we both do a little dance in the end zone.

"Fucking hell, best play all day," Cooper says, shaking his head at me the entire way back to the sidelines.

"Finally got a touchdown for your girl, Siska?" Coach Iverson asks, shaking his head. "I swear, you two." He tries to hide his smile, but he knows it was an awesome play.

I look up at the stands and find Adeline smiling. She mouths, "way to go," and I tilt my head like I told her so. She laughs, and goddamn, she's so beautiful.

"Now you've gotten yourself on the Jumbotron," Cooper says.

I lift my gaze, and sure enough, there are our faces in a heart with Cupid shooting an arrow at us.

"Man, that co-parents-with-benefits thing doesn't seem confusing at all."

I sit down next to Cooper, not interested in his opinion. We know what we're doing.

———

The Grizzlies win, and I end up scoring another touchdown, so our small group decides to go out and celebrate. Adeline's mom takes Clover back to her house for the night, and I cancel Haze for tomorrow morning.

We score VIP tickets, so we're in the

upper part of a nightclub with only a few other groups of people. Adeline and Bryce are dancing while I'm sitting and drinking a beer with Miles and Cooper. Ellery returns from the bathroom and joins the two women.

The dress Adeline borrowed from Bryce is probably going to get me into a fight tonight. It's tight and red, pushing her tits up and her ass out, which looks ready to be slapped. I've had to keep my dick in check more than once tonight.

Miles's eyes widen. "You look like a lion ready for his next steak."

"Fuck off." I finish my beer and slide out of the booth. I walk up to Adeline, grabbing her hand. "Come on."

"Where?"

"We're dancing."

"Really?" she shouts over the music.

I'm not a huge nightclub kind of guy. Peeper's Alley is definitely more my vibe, but when Bryce suggested we go to the nightclub, I was excited to see what Adeline would wear and that I'd have the excuse to dance with her.

The song changes to one with a slower

beat, one you could slow dance to if you wanted, which I do. I pull Adeline to me, my hands landing on her hips. Thank God for that agreement last night, because if I couldn't touch her in this dress, I'd go insane.

"You're good with your hands. Two touchdowns. I don't think I told you congratulations," she whispers in my ear, and her breath tickles my skin.

I pull her closer still, and she moans, causing my dick to harden further in my slacks.

"Pretty soon I'm going to show you how good I am with my hands when I sneak you off to the bathroom and make you watch me rub one out from how hot you look in that dress."

She grinds against my length.

"You're only making it worse."

She grins up at me. "Maybe we should've stayed at home." Her breasts press into my chest.

"Come on, you two. Let's dance," Bryce says over the music before she tugs Miles out onto the dance floor.

I'm so mesmerized by Adeline that I

didn't even realize the music tempo had gone up.

Adeline turns around and grinds her ass into my cock.

"Not helping, woman." But my fingers dug into her hips, and I thrust, grinding my length into her.

She straightens her back, her arms going up and fiddling with the short hair on the back of my head. She turns to look at me, and I take her mouth in a fierce kiss, my hands leaving her hips for her tits.

She groans and ends our kiss. "Take me somewhere."

"Home?"

Adeline shakes her head. "I don't care. Anywhere. I'm feeling naughty."

She does not have to tell me twice. I take her hand and tug her down a hallway. Damn, this is not how I ever wanted it to be with Adeline, but she's got me way too wound up.

A bouncer sits by the back door, and I motion to him that we want out. He steps aside, and we head out into the alley. I don't wait for Adeline to say anything, turning and pressing her against the brick wall. My lips collide with hers, thrusting my tongue deep into her mouth, not able to get enough of the taste of her.

My hand slides under the hem of her dress, and I groan into her mouth when I find her panties soaking wet. Sliding over the elastic hem, I run my finger up and down her swollen lips. "Come on, baby, get off on my fingers."

"I want to taste you." She squirms, and my fingers fall away.

She puts her hands on my shoulders and turns me so that my back is at the wall. She starts to move down to her knees, but there's zero chance I'm letting a prize like Adeline kneel on this dirty cement.

"Hold up." I quickly pull off my jacket and drop it on the ground between us. "There. Now please, continue."

"Prince Charming," she says with no small amount of sarcasm.

With a smile, she drops to her knees and stares up at me while I wrap my palm around her chin, loving the view. She fiddles with my belt, my button, and by the time she slides down my zipper, my dick is barely able to stay contained in my boxers.

Her delicate hands slide in and pull out my cock. She doesn't waste any time, licking the tip, teasing me as her other hand holds the weight of me at my base. My head rocks back against the wall, and I force myself to keep my eyes on her when she engulfs me in her mouth.

"Adeline, you're ruining me." I caress her face as she takes me deeper and deeper.

Once my tip hits the back of her throat, she swallows, her throat pressing against all angles of my cock, and I almost come in her mouth that instant. She works me over the best I've ever had, making me forget we're in a filthy alley outside a nightclub. My dick hardens even more in her mouth, and she doesn't stop sucking and licking and pumping me.

"I'm gonna come," I warn her, but she only makes a sound of affirmation, continuing to pleasure me.

The fact she's going to swallow sends me over the edge. I pump into her mouth until I come so hard I fear I might blackout.

"Holy shit, that was a religious experience."

She cleans me with her tongue and tucks

me back into my pants. I pull her up and wrap my hand around the back of her neck, kissing her with everything I'm feeling, tasting myself on her tongue.

"Time to go home." I bend and pick up my jacket, taking her hand, and head to the street to flag down a cab.

She giggles. "What about the others?"

"They're all adults. We have an empty apartment, and our baby isn't there to disturb us. Why would we stay at a club?"

A cab stops, and I open the door, practically shoving her into it. I just hope I can keep my hands off her until we get inside our apartment because she's quickly becoming an obsession.

CHAPTER 25

ADELINE

It's already mid-season, and Thanksgiving is almost here. Clover is growing so fast, I want time to slow down. She's laughing and smiling and eating well. She's a happy child, and I hope that's because of Damon and me being able to coexist even if we're not a couple.

That topic couldn't be more complicated now. I sleep solely in his bed, where we have sex almost every night except when he's gone for away games. There are the other times too, when Clover goes down for a nap and he traps me on the couch. Or when my mom insists on taking Clover for the night and we sit around practically naked and order in takeout.

The problem now is that it *feels* as if we're a couple, but we haven't had a conversation about it. Neither of us has confessed how we feel about the other, though it seems obvious in our actions.

I'm upstairs at Bryce's place because Damon has asked me to go out to dinner with him, and I need to borrow something. He told me he has something he wants to tell me tonight, and I want to make sure I look good. I had plans to go shopping, but Clover caught a cold earlier this week, and I couldn't take her out with me.

Tonight is also Miles and Bryce's first time babysitting Clover.

"I sure hope Damon's got his shit together, and he's going to confess his undying love for you tonight," she says to me from inside the walk-in closet. She comes out holding a gorgeous black dress that wraps to one side, leaving a nice slit in the middle. "This is the one."

"I love it," I gush because it's perfect.

"Great! Try it on."

I take the dress and go into their bathroom. Miles is downstairs with Damon, and I can only imagine the level of instructions Damon's giving him on taking care of Clover. I feel bad for Miles.

I don't want to say anything to Bryce, but I feel the same as her. I hope that whatever Damon's reason for taking me out tonight, it has something to do with us. At first, I was really scared at how close we were becoming, but my feelings have become too strong to turn back now without knowing what we could be. There's no denying that I want to be with him as more than just his co-parent or baby mama. I want to be on his arm as his girlfriend. I want us to commit to each other.

I emerge from the bathroom, and Bryce claps, smiling wide. "Perfect. You're going to leave him speechless. Do you have heels?"

I nod.

"I'm so excited for you. With Miles, I was more the idiot, like Damon. But Miles won me over, and I couldn't deny how I felt anymore. I hope Damon has come to his senses like I had to."

"I have no idea why he wants to have dinner," I remind her because I'm trying not to get my hopes up. Maybe he's really had it with Haze and wants us to find a new nanny.

"Stop being so pessimistic. Come on, let's get you guys going."

We walk down the cement steps, laughing about this boy in my class who asked me if Damon and I play catch a lot at home. Of course, Bryce had some way to make the comment sound dirty.

When we enter, it's just as I guessed—Damon is telling Miles everything about Clover. "Here is her pediatrician's number, but go to the ER if it's bad. And I don't mean Ellery, I mean go to the actual hospital."

"I'm sure we'll be fine." Bryce says, sliding her arm around Miles's waist.

"Don't feed her more than what we listed. You call us if you have any questions." Damon points at him.

"No, don't call us." I shake my head.

Damon finally notices me. His gaze roams up and down my body, and every nerve ending in me flares to life. His tongue licks his bottom lip. "Damn, you look stunning, Adeline."

"Thank you." I take in his suit. I think

this one is new. It's a tighter, slimmer fit and shows off how broad he is and how strong his thighs are. "Same to you."

I come up alongside him, and he takes my chin in his hand and bends down, placing a kiss on my lips. I'll never tire of that. And this is where lines are blurring lately. Used to be that we'd only be affectionate when and if we were going to sleep together. But for the past month, he'll kiss me goodbye when I leave in the morning or come up behind me if I'm cooking and hug me just to do it, not because it's going to lead anywhere. And now he's being affectionate in front of his friends. What does that mean? Hopefully after tonight, it will all be cleared up in my mind.

"Now you two get going. We have it all taken care of." Bryce turns around. "Where is the cutie anyway?" She finds Clover on the floor on her new play mat and rushes over to her, falling to her knees right before she reaches the baby.

"Damn, I thought she was going to fall on top of her," Damon says, staring at me with an expression to say maybe this is a bad idea.

"I have to get my heels." I go into the other bedroom where my clothes are still housed. We don't share a closet or a dresser, but that doesn't seem weird given all the square footage. So what if nothing of mine is in his room?

I slip into my heels and laugh when I notice Clover's pajamas set out for them with step-by-step instructions on how bedtime works.

"Let's go," I say when I leave the room, eager to get out of here.

Damon is watching Miles and Bryce interact with Clover. His hands are in his pockets and his jaw is clenched, his throat tense.

I come up next to him. "Are you ready?"

He looks down at me, and a smile forms on his lips. "Yeah. The sooner we're gone, the sooner this experiment is over."

"My mom couldn't babysit, and it's good experience for them. They're our friends and love her just as much as we do."

"Doubtful." He grabs my jacket from the coat hook, and I slide my arms into it.

"Have fun, you two." Bryce waves with

the clear impression she hopes for good news when we return.

I'm not looking for a ring or anything, but a declaration that he has feelings for me and wants to officially be in a relationship would be nice.

We say goodbye to Clover and head out to where a car is waiting for us at the curb. The driver gets out and opens the door for us. I slide in first, and Damon joins me, his thigh pressing against mine.

"Where are we going?"

He leans in close, his nose running up and down my jawline, inhaling my scent. "It's a surprise. You smell amazing, by the way."

Damon has no idea how intoxicating he is when he does things like that. He slides his hand in mine, running his thumb over my knuckles. I feel some scabs and scrapes on his hand from the last few games.

"How are your hands?" I ask.

He stares at our interlocked fingers. "Better."

We don't have to drive too long before the car stops in front of an expensive-looking restaurant. Damon files out first and holds his hand out to help me from the car. I step out, and he wraps his arm around my waist, holding me to him as if I'm his. No man has ever made me feel the way he does.

I'm not worried about the press photographing us. I think we're old news now. After they got enough pictures of Damon with Clover, they seemed to have moved on to more interesting things—like the football star whose brother is in trouble with the law.

When we get inside, he tells the hostess his last name, and it doesn't even bother me when her eyes take him all the way in. I'm at his side. I'm the one he wants. Now I'm getting turned on thinking about that.

She shows us to a small table for two tucked away in a dark corner. There's a box sitting on my seat when we arrive, and I look at it.

Damon is quick to pick it up, waiting for me to sit before placing it in my lap. "It's a gift."

"I do love gifts. But it's not my birthday."

"Just something I wanted to give you." He folds himself into the seat across from me. "Go ahead and open it."

I suck in a deep breath to keep my excitement and nerves at bay, then untie the blue bow on top and lift off the top of the box, smiling immediately. It's a Grizzlies jersey with the number twenty-three on it. I pick it up and turn it around to see SISKA over his number.

"Bryce wears Miles's, and Ellery wears Cooper's. You should wear mine."

I smile and clasp it to my chest. "Thank you. I'll wear it this weekend."

"Good." He nods. "There's something else in the box."

I dig past another layer of tissue paper and find a onesie with twenty-three and SISKA on the back.

"For whenever we feel comfortable with her coming to the games."

Who knows? If she keeps being that happy little girl, maybe I'll get her a set of headphones and bring her with me.

The waitress comes over, and Damon orders us an expensive bottle of wine. Once we've looked over the menu and ordered, sipping our wine after it's been delivered, Damon fidgets in his seat.

We chat for a bit about nothing of consequence until his obvious nerves make me anxious, so I finally ask, "You okay?"

"Yeah." He raises his wineglass as though he wants to give a toast, so I raise mine as well. "I just really wanted to thank you for moving down here during the season. These past few months have been so great for me, having Clover here every morning and most nights. I know the commute for you is hellish, so I wanted to take you to dinner to show you how much I appreciate it, appreciate you. I know if you hadn't agreed to move down here, I wouldn't have the bond I have with her today." He clinks his glass with mine, then sips from it.

I sip mine and slowly lower my glass to the table.

There has to be more, but he's no longer fidgeting. In fact, he seems much more relaxed. As if he can enjoy himself now that he's got that off his chest.

"Sorry if I seemed weird. I just hate talking about feelings. I wanted it to come out right." He sips his wine again, smiling wide, the perfect portrait of relaxed elegance.

I sit there, unsure what to do. I'd been hoping for a declaration of his feelings for me, but he's arranged this entire night to essentially thank me for living in his apartment rent-free and letting him fuck me every day. He's thanking me for being a full-service co-parent with perks and allowing him to be around his baby girl all the time.

"That's it?" I ask, my eyes on the fancy tablecloth.

"What?" he asks.

My gaze floats up to his. "That's it? That's what tonight is about? You thanking me for commuting to work so you can see your daughter whenever you're home? How about thanking me for the free pussy, why stop at just the commute?"

"Adeline…" He glances around.

"God, when will my gut steer me right? You're still *that* Damon."

"That Damon?" He sits up straighter and looks around again because I'm probably causing a scene, but I don't really care.

"The guy who would bring me to dinner but think about fucking the hostess."

He glances back toward the front of the restaurant. "I don't wanna fuck her."

Tears well up in my eyes, but there's zero chance I'm going to let him see them. "Do you really not feel it? Or are you just ignoring it? Are you that afraid of commitment?"

"I'm not sure what you're talking about." He reaches over to grab my hand, but I pull it away, fisting my hands in my lap.

"I love you," I say. "Do you really not know that?"

The color drains from his face. "Adeline… we're having fun. We agreed that it was just sex, that it didn't mean anything." He lowers his voice and leans over the table.

"Yeah, I did agree to that like an idiot, because if I'm honest with myself, I was probably already falling in love with you before I ever slept with you that night."

He shakes his head, panic lacing his features. "No. We're doing this for Clover. Co-parenting better than anyone we know. This was never about love or commitment. My only commitment is to Clover."

I shut my eyes, and the tears spill down. I nod and open them, meeting his horrified gaze. "And I'm thankful you're so committed to our daughter, but it turns out I'm just a fool. Have a fun lonely life, Damon." I get up from the chair, tossing the napkin on the table. He stands, but I put my hand on his chest. "Don't worry, I'll never keep Clover from you. You're a wonderful father, but I can see now that you're never going to be a wonderful partner. I can't play the game anymore. Goodbye, Damon."

"What? I don't understand," he whisper-shouts.

I turn back to him. He's so devastatingly handsome my heart splits wide open. "And that's the problem."

I wind through the tables and out of the restaurant, jogging a block with tears streaming down my face before I catch a cab back to our… er… his apartment.

CHAPTER 26

DAMON

Driving out to Adeline's, my gut twists. I've had two away games back to back, so I haven't seen Clover. But this is our new normal, so I might as well get used to it. This is co-parenting now, I guess.

I pull into her driveway and see a sedan already there. Great, she has company, and I don't even recognize the car. That tight feeling in my chest starts up again, and I swallow the feeling down the same way I have every other time I've thought about Adeline the past couple weeks. It only hurts if I let it hurt.

Walking up the sidewalk, I see that she

has some Christmas decorations up now—garland on the railing of the front porch and a cartoon Santa character plastered to the storm door. I ring the doorbell, and my nerves set in. How will Adeline react when she sees me? Hell, how will I react?

We never talked about what happened after that dinner. I didn't go home right away, and from what Bryce said, Adeline came in, packed a suitcase, and left with Clover. Bryce currently isn't talking to me, but it's none of her damn business.

Adeline opens the door and gives me a cold smile. That fucking smarts, and the tight feeling in my chest is back.

"She's almost ready to go. You can come in for a minute. I'll finish packing her a bag." She heads upstairs, where Clover must be.

I just want to see my daughter and hold her. I've missed her so much. Memories of bringing Clover home from the hospital to here, cooking dinners, the late-night feedings, the pacing back and forth with her in my arms to quiet her down all come rushing back. Adeline would sit on the stairs in her pajamas, watching me as we'd take shifts trying to soothe her.

"That should be it, Adeline." Henry comes out of the kitchen with a drill and screwdriver in his hands.

I swallow the lump in my throat. What the hell is he doing here?

"Oh, hey, Damon."

"Henry." I nod and push my hands into my pockets so they don't accidentally strangle him.

The doorbell rings, and I move toward the door, but Henry quickly goes over, setting his tools on the front table, and takes a package from a delivery guy. He moves some of the mail on the table and sets down the package, setting the envelopes on top.

Well, she's moved on fast.

Henry must see something on my face. "It's not what you think. I came to apologize for some shit I said when she was pregnant, and she asked if I could help her with some childproof locks in the kitchen."

I shrug, trying to disguise my relief. "I didn't ask."

"Although, I have to say you're the stupidest man on Earth. What more could you possibly want than Adeline? I mean, I get that you can have any pussy you want out there, but Adeline, man." He shakes his head. "One day you'll regret losing her."

"So you just gunning to slide into my place?" I arch an eyebrow.

He chuckles. "No, she doesn't want me. But one day, she'll find some lucky son of a bitch she does. And you'll show up like you did tonight to pick up your daughter, having to confront the lucky bastard who gets to be in Adeline's bed every night. The guy who gets to hold her and make her feel safe. The guy who gets to love her—and your daughter. And you'll walk out of the house, have a good weekend with your daughter, and when you drop her off, you'll go back to your empty big condo or mansion, wishing you could turn back time." He smacks me on the back. "You've got so many people who worship you, but I feel bad for you because to give up Adeline?" He shakes his head again. "You gave up the best thing you ever had."

"Thanks for the advice," I say through clenched teeth. It's taking every bit of control I have not to deck this guy.

Thankfully, Adeline comes down the stairs, so I don't have to continue this conversation with this idiot any longer. "I'm sorry, Henry. I just had to finish getting Clover's things together."

"No problem. I'm going to put these tools back where I found them in the basement. See you, Damon." He heads downstairs, but I don't bother saying goodbye to him. Good riddance is more like it.

Adeline hands me the bag. "Here you go. We just put her in the carrier. Do you want the stroller too?"

"No, I bought double of everything."

She winces. "Sorry, sounds so final," she admits.

It does. I just figured this way when we switch, it would be easier. "Sorry."

"Oh no, it's easier that way, and you have the means, so… good idea."

I take her hand. She allows me, but it's dead weight and limp in mine. "No, I meant I'm sorry for what happened. I wish—"

She shakes her head and takes her hand back. "It's fine, Damon. I romanticized it. I'll survive, believe me."

I would love to talk to her, but I'm not sure what I would even say. Even if I tried being with her, I'd only end up hurting her down the road, and that would be so much worse.

"I'll grab her so you can go." She turns and walks back up the stairs.

All I want to do is take Adeline's hips in my hands, step into her, and smell her, but she's not mine. She never was, and I need to remember that.

She returns with Clover. "Not sure if you're doing anything Christmassy with her, but I packed a holiday dress for her. It's in the bag. I figure you're just going back to The Den now, so she's in her pajamas in case she falls asleep in the car."

I close my eyes at her choice of words for the building. "Thanks."

"Sure. I think my mom is going to pick her up on Friday while I'm at work and bring her back here. Still have Haze?" Her voice is all wrong. It's detached and monotone.

"No."

"Can't say I'm surprised."

"Actually, he said he couldn't afford to only work half the time since she won't be there every day, so he found another family. There will be a new nanny. She's older, Mrs.

Doubtfire type. Since I won't have her all the time, it works out."

She nods. "I'm glad."

Our eyes catch, and for a second, I want to beg her to come back to the city with me.

"I'll see you out." She leans in and kisses Clover. "See you in a few days, sweetie. Have fun with Daddy!"

I don't miss the false excitement in Adeline's voice or the tears in her eyes. Probably because she hasn't been away from Clover like this ever before. I hate that I'm the cause, but this is our new normal. We might as well get used to it.

I take the bag, put Clover in her carrier, and walk out of the house.

Henry must have slunk out the back door because he's outside, putting something in the trunk of his car.

I stop and lean in when I pass him. "It's not your fucking house. Go play Mr. Fix-It somewhere else. And no matter how hard you try, she'll never love you like she did me."

I'm pissed off and taking it out on a guy who'd probably treat Adeline the way she deserves.

Fuck, Bryce is right. I am a total bastard.

———

It's our one day off, and I'm just getting back from the store with Clover. When I get to my apartment, I find two big, annoying football players waiting on my landing for me.

Cooper takes the carrier from me. "I'll take my goddaughter, thank you." He reaches in and tickles her, and Clover laughs.

"What are you guys doing here?" I ask as I set down the grocery bag and unlock the door.

"We're your conscience," Miles says.

They follow me into the apartment and look around.

"Looks like a baby store threw up in here. Why do you still have some of Adeline's things out?" Cooper asks, giving Miles a look as he sets down the carrier.

"Yeah, just a heads-up, I'll probably be moving out of The Den next season. There isn't enough room for Clover here." I take her out of her carrier.

Again, the two of them share a look.

Cooper grabs Clover from me, putting her between his legs on the floor and pulling out some of her toys. The man is desperate for me to say he's her godfather.

"Go ahead, give me the speech. Nothing is going to change." I sit on my couch.

"How can you still be in denial?" Miles asks, taking the seat across from me. "You're hurting everyone. You, Adeline, Clover…"

"And fucking Bryce." I roll my eyes. "Spare me the lecture just so your fiancée can be happy."

"Shit," Miles says, sounding exasperated. "He's already too far gone."

"It's a slippery slope," Cooper says. "We came too late."

"Shut the fuck up." I scowl at them both.

Cooper covers Clover's ears. "Hey now, no using that language around my god-daughter."

I roll my eyes again. "What do you want me to say? That I love Adeline? I'm inca-pable of that emotion."

"Bullshit. You love Adeline," Miles says.

"I love that little girl." I point at Clover. "Sure, I cared for Adeline. We had a lot of fun, and I never would've thought we'd mesh that well together. She's awesome, and I'm glad she's Clover's mom, but I'm not husband material."

"Why?" Cooper asks. He's rarely the serious one, that's Miles's role in this friend group, so I'm thrown for a second.

"Why what?"

"Why aren't you husband material? Because you fucked a bunch of jersey chasers and earned a reputation? Hello, you're not alone in that. There's something you haven't told us, something that has you giving up everything that matters in your life." Cooper puts a block toy in front of Clover, and she stares at him like "who are you?" "I'm your godfather," he says as if Clover knows the word.

"There's nothing you don't know," I lie because I'm not going to get into the whole Greta thing right now. Even if they knew, it wouldn't change how I feel.

"Everyone can change," Miles says. "Look at Lee."

"Lee was always big on relationships. I'm the one who fucked it up for him with Shayna in college."

Miles looks up as if he doesn't remember,

then nods, remembering that it was my fault. See? I don't only ruin my own relationships, I ruin other people's too. I'm one helluva guy.

"Okay, then, I'm arguing that it was obvious you loved her by the way you looked at her. There was love there," Cooper says. "And it's different than when you look at this little one. You wanted Adeline to be yours. You enjoyed your little family of three, and you loved it when she felt like yours even if you guys didn't put a label on it. Until you did that whole restaurant stunt."

I stand up, my frustration boiling over. "I fucking took her to thank her! I didn't know she'd fallen in love with me."

"Then you're fucking blind!" Miles says, standing up too. "You know what I think? I think Peter Pan doesn't want to fucking grow up. You're not just messing your life up now, Damon." He points at Clover. "Look at her. She doesn't know it now, but what's going to happen in five, ten, hell, twenty years from now when she grows up and realizes that her dad can't be intimate with anyone? And to be clear, when I use the word intimate, I'm not talking about sex."

I hold up my hand. "Okay, I get that you're smarter than me, but I'm not a fucking dumbass. I knew what you meant by intimate."

"You didn't know that Adeline was in love with you. How did we all fucking know, but you didn't?"

Cooper covers Clover's ears again. "Hello, language. We don't want her first word to be the f-word."

"I'm not sure what you want from me?" I throw my arms in the air.

"I want you to look inside and figure out where the block is and do some work on it. Because this guy, this Damon Siska, he's not anyone I would want to know. You were the best version of yourself when you were with Adeline. Your daughter deserves that. *You* deserve that. Life is hard enough, but to purposely deny yourself happiness... I don't get it." Miles shakes his head. "I'm sorry, I can't be here anymore. Ruin your fucking life for all I care."

"Again, language!" Cooper says.

"Fuck off, Coop!" Miles shouts at him.

The door slams, and Clover's bottom lip quivers before she cries.

"Damn him." I pick her up. "It's okay, baby. It's okay."

Cooper stands. "This was all really en-lightening. You know he's only pissed be-cause it's hard to see someone throw away their happiness. He fought really hard to get Bryce, and she did a lot of healing to meet him halfway." When I don't say anything, he goes on. "Just so I know, your goal in life is to die alone?"

I still don't say anything.

"Cool, then. Don't worry, I'll be there to console my goddaughter."

"Fuck you, Coop."

"Talk some sense into your daddy. No one wants to die alone." He runs his hand on her back since she's still upset. "I'm out."

He leaves the apartment, and I really wish everyone would just stay the hell out of my business. I know what's best, and this is it.

CHAPTER 27
ADELINE

When I pull into my driveway, I see a dark-windowed sedan parked in front of my house. Who the hell is this? Is Damon filing custody papers against me? These last couple of days without Clover have been even more unbearable than the two weeks before without Damon.

I park my car and get out, waiting for the person in the back seat to emerge. My voice locks down when I see Stanley Siska.

I close my eyes.

"Good evening, Adeline," he says. "I'm sorry for dropping in on you like this, but I felt what I needed to discuss with you should be done face-to-face."

"Okay, would you like to come in?"

"I would love to, thank you."

I unlock my door, and he steps in after me. "Sorry, Clover is with Damon this week."

"I'm aware. Heather is with them now. Damon isn't aware I'm in town. He believes his mom came on her own."

"Okay…" That's weird. "Coffee? Tea?"

"Just a water is fine. Thank you." He sits at my kitchen table and pulls out some papers.

Great. Fucking papers. I knew it.

"If that's a custody agreement, I will have you know that I don't have nearly the money you do, but I will find a way to fight for my daughter. You cannot take her away from me."

He sighs. "I would never, and I'm embarrassed that I ever gave you the impression I would take your daughter from you. Please sit." He holds out his hand, and I slide into the chair across from him. "The way I treated you at the shower wasn't kind, and I apologize. You are both grown adults and have every right and ability to make your own decisions without me inserting myself. It's just…" He stares off for a moment. "Damon was our easy child. He did what he was supposed to all the time. Worked his ass off to play pro, and we couldn't be prouder of him in that regard. But there was a life-altering event that happened to him in high school. It's not my story to tell, but his mother and I believe that one horrible thing changed him. We tried to get him counseling, but he refused. Said he was able to deal with it on his own."

I'm dying to know what the heck he's talking about.

"I'm not sure what happened between you and Damon. All Heather and I were told by our son was you'd moved out and you two would be sharing custody. He only told us because Heather wanted to know about the holidays. Knowing him, he wouldn't have told us otherwise. He's kept people at arm's length ever since…"

"That's not it. He just doesn't love me, Mr. Siska."

He chuckles. "If you think my son doesn't love you, you're as blind as he is."

I say nothing, and he takes a sip of his water.

"Let me get back to what I was saying. When Damon told us he got a one-night stand pregnant, I wasn't surprised. And I wasn't happy. His lifestyle was bound to catch up to him. But, and I do not say this to sound like an ass, we have money. Damon has a lot of money between his trust and his salary with the Grizzlies, not to mention his endorsements. There are women out there who would want a piece of it. But you're not that type, are you?"

"No, I'm not."

"I can assure you, I don't think you are." He chuckles again. "And because of that, I brought these papers. This is Clover's trust, and there are now only two people who can control it until she turns of age." He slides the papers toward me, where it shows Damon Siska listed as father and Adeline Morgan listed as mother. "It's set up for her to access when she's twenty-five. I did put a stipulation that I'd like her to go to college before she's to get it. She'll have enough in an account that Heather and I will make for her to pay for college."

"You don't have to do that. The trust is more than she'll ever need. Damon and I will figure something out."

Though I was hesitant about the trust fund at first, it's a good feeling to know your daughter will one day be so well taken care of financially. Not that she'll know anything about it until she's twenty-four and three-quarters years old.

"She's our grandchild, and I fear she'll be our only one if my son keeps denying his feelings."

"Thank you. It means a lot to me that you trust me to be in charge of it for her. I would never touch that money."

"I know. I'd offer you money, but I'm pretty sure you wouldn't take anything from me."

"You're right, I wouldn't."

He sips his water again. "I'm going to apologize for my son. I do hope his decision to let you go was a lapse in judgment and he comes to his senses, because I've only ever once before seen him look at a woman remotely close to the way he looks at you. And it's so much stronger with you. He does love you, so even if you don't work out because he's too lost, I hope you find some peace in knowing that."

I give him a small smile. "Thanks."

He stacks the papers and puts them in the center of the table. "We'll need to have these signed in front of lawyers, but I'll leave a copy for you to look over. Thank you for letting me barge in." He stands and looks around my small house. "You two really made quite a home here for you three."

I don't say anything for fear that the rawness crawling up my throat will result in me crying on his shoulder.

He's about to leave when I stop him. "Please, Mr. Siska, can you tell me what happened?"

"Damon will kill me, but he should've told you himself. Google Greta Mackey. Connecticut. Accident. It should come up."

My stomach drops. "Thank you."

"The reason I want you to know is because us Siska men are shitty at displaying our emotions and turning them into words. I'm really happy you're my granddaughter's mother, Adeline. She's going to have one helluva role model growing up."

Now I am crying. I wipe the tears. "Thank you, and have a safe trip back."

The minute Mr. Siska's car pulls away from the curb, I grab my laptop from my bag and type in all the information he told me to. The old article pops up right away.

Young Connecticut Woman Dies on Vermont Slopes.

I continue reading. Greta was skiing and fell, hitting her head in a way they refer to as blunt force trauma. She was with her boyfriend, although they don't say his name because he was a minor. They transported her by airlift to a hospital, but there was a lot of internal bleeding, and she passed away hours later. Her parents weren't able to make it to her bedside fast enough, which left the boyfriend there on his own. The family referred to him as her one true love and said they were happy he could be there when she passed on.

More tears stream down my face.

Oh, Damon, why did you never tell me?

Because I wasn't important enough, that's why.

CHAPTER 28

DAMON

've been in a bad mood since I woke up. Miles and Cooper's words keep echoing through my head and wearing me down, pushing me closer to admitting my feelings for Adeline. But no good can come from that.

Clover is napping, and Adeline's mom will be here any minute to pick her up. I hate having to send her away.

Miles's words float through my head about how I need to figure this shit out. He has a point, I suppose.

I grab the box in the corner of my closet and open it on my bed. A picture of Greta and me is the first thing I see. Then her homecoming corsage, movie tickets, all the stuff she kept in a memory box her parents gave me after she died. She even had all the small notes I'd dropped into her locker.

The pain surfaces immediately, the memories of her lying on the snow. I'd begged her to go for another run down the hill when she'd wanted to go in. The life flight, the hospital, the look in the doctor's eyes when he told me to call her parents. Her hand going limp in mine, and the nurse coming in to shut off the machine.

I rub my hand over my heart, trying to soothe the pain.

My buzzer goes off, and I fumble to put the lid on the box and shove it under my bed for now. I let Adeline's mom in, then open my apartment door.

Picking up Clover, I cradle her before putting her in the carrier, buckling her up. "I'm gonna miss you so much, sweet girl."

"Hello?" Marge peeks her head in.

"Hey, I'm just getting her in the car seat. If you're lucky, she'll sleep on the way back." I try to keep my voice light.

She smiles. "Actually, while she's sleeping, I was hoping I could talk to you."

Fuck, this will be fun, hearing a bunch of "I told you so's" and "You're not good enough for my daughter." Tell me something I don't know.

"Sure, do you want to sit?" I motion to the living area.

"I'd love to."

We go over to the couch, and she sits. "You're none of my business, but my daughter is my business and my granddaughter is my business, so I'm just going to shoot it straight. Your dad visited Adeline last night."

I drop down on the other end of the couch. I fucking knew it was bullshit when my mom showed up here out of nowhere saying she missed her granddaughter. "And?"

"I hate to bring up a subject you obviously don't like to talk about, but he mentioned a name to her. Greta?"

Anger pours through my blood like burning lava. "He shouldn't have. It's none of his business."

"That's where you're wrong, Damon."

"Excuse me?" I don't want to be rude to Adeline's mom, but I'm done with everyone saying they know what's best for me.

"It became my business and your father's business the minute you got my daughter pregnant."

"Okay, but—"

She puts up her hand to stop me. "You invited my daughter into your life, and I understand that you went through something traumatic at such a young age, but I'm here to tell you—and I realize I didn't know her—but if Greta did love you, she wouldn't want you to throw your life away with different women who mean nothing to you. Because if she wanted that for you, then that's not love, Damon. Love is wanting the other person to be happy, regardless of where that puts you. A partner's love…" She shakes her head. "I don't think I have to explain it to you because I saw you, Damon. I saw you love my daughter, and you love her fiercely."

I look down at my hands, unable to look her in the eye. She'll see the truth.

"Now tell me, why are you so hell-bent on denying that love? Because I fear that you're confusing love for guilt. That your guilt over what happened to Greta has eaten you up over the years, and you've convinced yourself that you never want to go through that loss again."

"Why the hell would I ever want to experience that pain again?" My voice is raw. I still can't look at her.

"That's valid. No one likes to have their heart broken. No one likes to lose love. But if you ask anyone who's lost someone they loved whether they'd change things and never have had that love in their life, most people would rather have had what little time they could get with that person."

"Why are you saying all this? You don't even like me."

She smiles. "I didn't like you much at first, that's no secret. But then I saw the effort you put in during the pregnancy and after Clover was born. And I watched my daughter fall in love with you. It's my job as a parent to get her what she wants. Which means me here, talking to you. Are you happy, Damon? Right now, have you been happy these past few weeks? Are you relieved to not have Adeline here?"

"Hell no." My face crumples and I let my head drop, my hands in my hair.

"Then why are you putting your family through this?" she asks softly.

I finally bring my head up and meet her eyes. "She's better off without me."

"That's bullshit, and you know it."

I put my head in my hands again. "Because I love her more than Greta. Is that what you want to hear? I love her with everything inside me, and if something happens to her…" I squeeze my eyes shut, shaking my head. "I'm not sure I could ever recover."

She pats my knee. "Oh, sweetie, everybody who has ever truly loved someone understands that fear, but while you're sitting here worried about something that might never happen, you're losing out on all the good moments. Take it from me, time goes so fast. One day you'll blink, and your little girl will be an adult, having her own baby. Somewhere on your way to becoming a pro athlete, you were able to put your fear aside. Find the same courage here. Don't miss out on all the good days you could have by worrying about the bad days that may never come."

"I miss Adeline," I whisper, fear and relief warring with each other at admitting it out loud.

"Guess what?" She dips her head to look at me, and I turn mine to the side. "There's a solution to that problem. Go get her back."

I pick up my head and look at the clock. "She's still in school. Shaylene will never let me through."

"You're the Chicago Grizzlies starting wide receiver. You're going to let little ol' Shaylene keep you from winning your woman back?"

She's right.

"Hell no." I stand and look around.

"How about I drive you?"

"Yeah, thanks."

I grab Clover's carrier, and we leave the apartment.

Damn, what if she doesn't take me back? Fuck that. I won her once. I can do it a second time. I won't quit trying until Adeline's back where she belongs.

———

When we park outside the middle school, I'm more nervous than I was before the championship game last year.

"I've got Clover. You go get in," Marge says.

I run up to the doors, press the button, and tap my foot.

"Hello, how can I help you?" Shaylene answers.

"I'm here to see Adeline Morgan," I say.

She buzzes me in, and I go straight into the office.

"You know I'm not letting you in, Mr. Siska. Elijah." Shaylene jots something on a piece of paper and waves for him to come over. "Give Miss Morgan this note."

"No!" I put my hand over the note.

In the meantime, Adeline's mom and Clover get buzzed in.

"Please, I really want to surprise her." I give Shaylene my best pleading face.

"I cannot let you through those doors."

I take everything out of my pockets and place it on the counter. My keys, gum, wallet. "You want me to strip? I will." I grab the hem of my shirt.

"Oh jeez," she says. "Please don't."

"Please do," another woman farther back in the office says.

"Let him in, Shaylene. He wants to confess his love to her," Adeline's mom says, coming up to my side.

Vic, the security guard, comes in, and I point at him. "He can walk me the entire way. I'll do anything. Please."

"Let him through," Elijah says, and I fist bump him.

"Oh, for heaven's sake." Vic reaches under her desk and presses the button for the doors into the school.

I run to grab the door, then turn around. "Where is her room?"

"I'll show you." Vic comes alongside me. "Does baby want to come too?"

Adeline's mom holds the carrier to me, but I grab it and take Marge's arm. "You got me here. You have to see how this ends."

She smiles at me. I think I earned some brownie points there.

"Vic, you better keep your eye out," Shaylene calls.

As we walk the halls, Clover's eyes

flutter open, and she smiles up at me as though she knows Daddy finally came to his senses. I just hope Mommy still loves me.

CHAPTER 29

ADELINE

"Please sit down, Lucy."

Today has been a constant challenge, getting the students to be quiet and stop talking or standing up from their desks when they're supposed to be working.

A commotion in the hallway piques their interest, and some of them rush over to the window that looks out into the hall.

"Please, you guys. I am tired of saying the same thing. Sit down."

"Miss Morgan!" Sydney says in an excited voice, turning to face me with her mouth open.

"I don't even want to know," I mumble.

After a quick rap on the door, Vic walks in and puts out his hand. "You have some visitors."

"But Shaylene didn't call to tell me, and I'm not expecting anyone." I sit at my desk, massaging my temples. My entire body hurts from barely sleeping and crying so much last night.

"She finally let me through."

Damon's voice has my head whipping up and looking over in his direction.

He walks in and sets Clover in her carrier on a desk.

"Damon?" My face must be filled with confusion right now.

He looks at the kid sitting at the desk where he set the carrier. "Are you old enough to babysit?"

Marcus gives him a look and shrugs.

"Okay then." Damon picks up the carrier and walks over to my desk.

I stand, and Clover smiles wide when she sees me. I can't help but smile back.

"Adeline, I was an idiot."

I return my focus to Damon. I have no idea what's going on here, and I'm almost afraid to hope.

"I was lost and in denial about how much I loved you. I should've told you at the restaurant that night, but I was so scared. You know about Greta, but I realize now that that's no good reason for me to put us through this. I was just so afraid to love you and lose you. You're everything to me, and these past two weeks have been gut-wrenching. I've been miserable and lashing out at everyone. I don't know how to be me anymore without you. Everything reminds me of you. I found a hair tie under the bed the other day, and I thought I might start crying. Or the smell of you on my sheets."

"OHHH!!!" the classroom roars.

"Keep it PG," I whisper to him.

"Please take me back, put me out of my misery. It would really make Clover happy too."

After thinking about what his dad said, I looked back and realized that Damon did love me. And everything he's saying here today is all I've wanted to hear from him. But I can't just rush back into his arms. I have to make him sweat it out, at least a little.

"You're going to use our daughter to try to get me back?"

"No, but it's the truth. I'll never hurt you like I did. I promise." His eyes are pleading.

"How can you promise that?" I round my desk, and he stares at my breasts that are snug in the middle school T-shirt I'm wearing for casual day.

"Because I've been schooled by a lot of people this week." He glances back at my mom. "And I might make mistakes, but I don't repeat them. But mostly, because I love you as much as I love our daughter, just in a different way." He winks, and I can't help the smile that lifts the corners of my mouth. "And if you decide you don't love me anymore, I'll be heartbroken, but I'll deal with it. If you need someone like Henry—"

"Eh… Mr. Ream? Miss Morgan, pick Damon."

I wave off Lucy.

"If you need a man like that, if he's what will make you happy, then I'll walk away. I don't want to, but what I want most is for you to be happy. So if I'm not enough or what you want, it's okay. All I want is for you to live a happy life." He looks back at my mom, and she nods.

Seriously, are these two besties now?

I cross my arms and jut out a hip. "The Damon Siska I know wouldn't think I could get over him in two weeks."

He shrugs. "Well, I don't think you have. But I really do just want you to be happy. I really want you happy with me. If you choose someone else, I might be put in prison for murder, so…"

I can't help but laugh, and even Clover laughs in her carrier.

"You hurt me. Don't ever do it again. You have to be open and transparent with me about your feelings going forward. Good or bad. Promise me."

The hope and relief in his eyes almost has me bursting into tears. "I promise you, Adeline. But be prepared, because you're going to have to listen to me talk a lot about how much I love you. It could get annoying."

I shake my head at him. "Now, tell me… how do you heal my hurt?"

He stares at me, and I walk toward him. He wraps his arm around my waist and pulls me to him. "I kiss it until you feel better?"

"You better believe it, and this hurt is going to take me a long time to recover from." I grin.

"I'd have it no other way." He places his lips on mine.

We try to keep it PG for the kids. There's a little tongue, but not too much. Don't want a bunch of parents calling me.

When I pull away, he rests his forehead on mine. "Thank you."

"For?" I pull away to look at him.

"Loving me. You fixed all those broken pieces inside me and made me whole again."

"Thanks for loving me back."

He kisses me again. Clover whines, and we both peer into her car seat.

Damon unstraps her and picks her up, bringing her into our hug. "I'm happy to have both my girls in my life again."

I give him a quick, chaste kiss.

"Funny, huh?" he asks.

"What?"

"We never found out who sent that text.

We really have them to thank for ending up here."

I roll my eyes. "I told you I was going to tell you anyway."

"But who knows? Maybe you would have, maybe you wouldn't. Whoever sent that text is the real reason we're standing here."

I look at my mom, and she's smiling so wide it makes me wonder. Truth is, there are a lot of people it could've been for a whole slew of reasons.

"I don't care how we got here, I'm just happy we did," I say.

"Me too." He takes my chin in his hands, tilting my head up. "I love you." He seals it with a gentle kiss that patches up all the bruises on my heart.

And Clover decides to take that special moment to, with one long grunt, have a blowout in her diaper.

"Eww!" the whole class shouts.

Damon and I just laugh.

Never a dull moment.

EPILOGUE

DAMON

"Whoa, Chicago, two years in a row!" Ronnie Michaels shouts into the microphone at the crowd as orange and blue confetti falls from the rafters. "We're thrilled to bring this home to you again!" He raises our championship trophy in the air.

Rip Klein, one of the sports commentators, comes to the microphone. "And we have one more trophy to give away—the MVP!"

The crowd goes crazy.

I'm not expecting to win MVP. I had a good game, but not outstanding like Miles did last year. That was some crazy shit.

Adeline finally reaches me in the crowd, clutching Clover. They're both wearing my jersey, and Clover's got on her pink headphones for the noise. "This is crazy! We barely got here, but I'm glad we did before they announced the MVP. Congratulations!"

I bend down and kiss her. "I've won enough this year."

"You played amazing, right, Clover?"

Clover gives me a sloppy kiss. She's nine months old already and has started being more mobile, having just learned to crawl.

"Definitely the luckiest guy in the world right here."

Rip clears his throat. "Here, Ronnie, go ahead and announce it." He hands the Grizzlies' GM a piece of paper.

"This guy, huh?" Ronnie says. "He's given me a lot of trouble over the years. Had to bail him out more than once. But he's one helluva player on the field, and I'm happy to say, this year, he finally got his life figured out, both on and off the field. Now he's got a beautiful woman and an adorable kid by his side. Damon Siska, everyone!"

Holy shit.

My stomach gets that roller-coaster-swooping while the crowd goes crazy again. I drag Adeline up to the stage with Clover in her arms. All my teammates pat me on the shoulders as I pass them.

Taking the trophy, I lean into the microphone. "I just told Adeline I had everything a man could want, but I will admit this makes this past year even sweeter. I love playing for Chicago, and I hope it never ends. Go Grizzlies! Thank you."

The crowd cheers, and I bring Adeline's lips to mine in a kiss I know will be broadcast to tens of millions of people.

Ronnie gets back on the microphone. "If there were any women out there thinking Damon Siska is still available, I think this is proof he's not."

As I kiss Adeline, a small hand lands on my cheek. I open my eyes to see Clover put her other hand on her mom's cheek, as though she wants us to keep kissing.

The crowd all awws and goes wild.

Isn't that just like a Siska, to steal the show? That's my good girl.

Instead of staying in town that night, we head back to Chicago with my parents on their plane. Bowl celebrations aren't made for babies, and the two people I want to celebrate with the most are with me.

My parents insisted on taking Clover to their rental after we landed to give us some time alone, so the next morning, I wake up alone with Adeline in my apartment.

We'll live in Adeline's house for the remainder of the school year, then she'll move into The Den permanently and find a job teaching in the city. After I retire, we'll move out of the city, but I don't think we'll stay in this apartment much longer. We need more space and a small yard since we plan on having more kids.

I roll over onto Adeline, using my thigh to separate her legs.

"Is this how you always plan on waking me up after I move back in?" she asks, her voice still a little groggy.

"I think so." The tip of my dick settles at her opening, and she scootches back.

"Unless you want another Clover, big guy, I suggest you put something on that thing."

"Since when is my dick a thing? And is another so bad?"

She holds up her left hand. "I gave you

the first one for free, but there will not be a second until there's a ring on this finger."

"I guess you mean a diamond ring, right?"

"Yes, and not one you win as a prize in one of those toy things." She chuckles.

I rest my head on her chest for a moment, then pick it up and look into her eyes. She looks worried now.

"That wasn't an ultimatum. I'm not asking for you to propose to me. I'm happy right where we are," she clarifies—probably because she knows that nowadays, I'd do anything to make her happy.

She says she wants me to jump, and I jump. I still have so much to make up for for being such an idiot. But she doesn't know everything like she thinks she does.

Like the fact that I planned for my parents to say they wanted Clover last night. Nor the fact that we're leaving today for a trip and Clover will go back to Connecticut with my parents. I already talked to Adeline's principal and made the arrangements for her to be off for a week. I'm really hoping she's excited about us going to the Caribbean and not upset that I took things into my own hands.

But first things first.

"So if I put a ring on that finger right now, I can fuck you without a condom?"

She stares at me and inhales. "Do you really want another one? Clover's not even one. I mean, two kids so close in age…"

I kiss her quickly and shrug a shoulder. "Maybe we'd get a boy."

"Is that what this is about? You want a boy?"

"Don't do that. I'm more than happy with my girls. I could be a girl dad to five, and I'd be thrilled. All right, since you seem so against it…" I stretch over the nightstand drawer and grab the box of condoms.

Rising to my knees, pretending I'm actually going to put one on, I open the box and pull out the case holding the large engagement ring I stashed there. I place it on her chest, open, so that the diamond sparkles.

"Damon!" Adeline slides up, and the box falls to the mattress.

"Okay, let's try that again." I chuckle and pick up the box and hold it out in front of her.

She looks at the diamond and then back at me. "Seriously?"

"Adeline, marry me. Let's make this official. I want to spend the rest of our lives together."

"Is this so you don't have to use a condom?" she asks, and I laugh.

"No, baby, that was just to get us here. We're using a condom because I'm not ready to share you with more than Clover right now." I lean forward and kiss her. "Marry me because you want to spend the rest of your life being spoiled by me, being loved by me."

"Well, I don't know… I have one condition." She smirks.

Adeline gets up out of bed and struts over to the closet. We've been making room for her things and getting rid of mine. I lie down, admiring the view of her naked body, until she puts on a hat from inside the closet and turns around.

"You need to get rid of these hats first." The trucker hat on her head says "Den Member" on it. Coming back over to the bed, she straddles my waist. "Found these the other day. Were they souvenirs for your conquests to take with them?"

I laugh. "We can keep one, right?"

"Why would we do that?" She arches an eyebrow.

I take her left ring finger and slide the diamond ring on because we both know she's going to say yes. "Because you were a Den Member and a mama bear before you were my wife. We can call it coming full circle."

She shakes her head and chuckles. "Why do you make it so hard to stay mad at you?"

"Because I'm adorable. Now, say the word I need to hear." I fiddle with the ring.

"My life would be nothing without you and Clover. Yes, of course I'll marry you."

I wind my hand around the back of her head and bring her lips down to mine. And then I grab a condom and make love to my fiancée.

———

Four hours later, I'm on an airplane with my parents, Adeline's parents, and Clover because Adeline's not ready to leave Clover for that long. But this way, everyone can have a vacation. I just put my foot down and insisted that we sleep by ourselves. Even if I know that probably won't happen, I'm okay with it.

We land, and my phone dings with a message from Miles. What the hell? He knows I planned to get away with Adeline for a week. Why is he messaging me?

Check this out.

He sends me a screenshot of a picture from the bowl game. It shows our teammate Bradley, the other wide receiver for the Grizzlies, all relaxed and leaning on a metal gate and talking to Ellery while Cooper talks to the press in the background.

Does Bradley know Ellery and Coop?

Don't think so since he's new to the team, but maybe this will force Cooper to actually make his move.

> We can only hope.

> I'll see you in two days.

He includes a winky emoji.

I turn to look at my fiancée as we approach the customs desk. "Adeline, why will Miles see me in two days?"

She gives me her sweet smile.

"Jesus, we're never going to be alone," I whine.

"I told you about foul language in front of the baby," Cooper says, joining us sans Ellery.

I give Adeline a pleading look. "Did everyone hijack our vacation?"

The End

COCKAMAMIE UNICORN RAMBLINGS

Oh, Damon. We will admit we are both fans of redeemed playboy hero but adding a baby in is like adding extra whipped cream to our sundaes. Damon with Clover… AW… ovaries exploding.

Luckily, we asked our group what they most loved about secret pregnancy tropes before we wrote this one and our faithful Unicorns made sure to comment with things we needed to have in there. While we probably haven't been able to include everything, hopefully you loved what we did manage to get in there!

Redeeming a playboy can be tricky and we had a lot of scenarios in our head as to why Damon couldn't or wouldn't settle down. We talked through things like his issues with his dad and his dad causing problems with a paternity test. We even talked about bringing another guy in (probably Henry) to cause conflict to push Damon to make his move. In the end, we wanted them to come from two good families who were protecting their kids. You saw how Adeline's mom with how she behaves with Damon in the beginning and Damon's dad thinking the worst of Adeline. The heartfelt moments at the end sealed our hearts for this family to come together.

Ultimately, Damon stood in his own way (as we all so often do) because of what happened when he was a teenager, and we think it fit their story. Did we want to hit Damon over his gorgeous head a few times? Yep! But in the end who hasn't known that person who sticks to what they believe almost stubbornly. We certainly have.

The hardest part of writing this book was the early chapters because they knew nothing about each other, other than that they were having a baby together. We wrote ourselves into a corner (one of many!) when we wrote the scene with them at the end of Miles book and it mentioned that he'd been hiding out from all of them. So, we couldn't bring the gang in until halfway through the book! UGH! It turned out for the best though because it gave these two a lot of time to get to know one another.

In the end, we love the way the story turned out. The three of them make such a happy little family and we can actually envision Clover wearing Damon's jersey in the stands, cheering on her daddy with her pregnant mommy in football seasons to come.

As always, we have a lot of people to thank for getting this book into your hands!

Nina and the entire Valentine PR team.
Cassie from Joy Editing for line edits.
Ellie from My Brother's Editor for line edits.
Rachel from My Brother's Editor for proofreading.
Hang Le for the cover and branding for the entire series.

All the bloggers who read, review, share and/or promote us.

The Piper Rayne Unicorns in our Facebook group who always think we score a touchdown! LOL

Every reader who took the time to read this book! Thank you for granting us your most precious resource—time. We don't take that lightly and appreciate it more than you'll ever know!

Coming next is Cooper. This friends to lovers book is sure to shock you with some surprising twists because after all these years, why haven't Cooper and Ellery stepped over the line of friendship? Find out in their book, Something like Love!

xo,
Piper & Rayne

ABOUT PIPER & RAYNE

Piper Rayne is a USA Today Bestselling Author duo who write "heartwarming humor with a side of sizzle" about families, whether that be blood or found. They both have e-readers full of one-clickable books, they're married to husbands who drive them to drink, and they're both chauffeurs to their kids. Most of all, they love hot heroes and quirky heroines who make them laugh, and they hope you do, too!

ALSO BY PIPER RAYNE

Chicago Grizzlies

On the Defense

Something like Hate

Something like Lust

Something like Love

The Nest

Mr. Heartbreaker

Mr. Broody

Mr. S (Title to be revealed)

Mr. C (Title to be revealed)

Kingsmen Football Stars

False Start

You Had Your Chance, Lee Burrows

You Can't Kiss the Nanny, Brady Banks

Over My Brother's Dead Body, Chase Andrews

Holiday Romances

Single and Ready to Jingle

Claus and Effect

Merry Kissmas

The Baileys

Lessons from a One-Night Stand

Advice from a Jilted Bride

Birth of a Baby Daddy

Operation Bailey Wedding (Novella)

Falling for My Brother's Best Friend

Demise of a Self-Centered Playboy

Confessions of a Naughty Nanny

Operation Bailey Babies (Novella)

Secrets of the World's Worst Matchmaker

Winning my Best Friend's Girl

Rules for Dating Your Ex

Operation Bailey Birthday (Novella)

Hockey Hotties

Countdown to a Kiss

My Lucky #13

The Trouble with #9

Faking it with #41

Tropical Hat Trick (Novella)

Sneaking around with #34

Second Shot with #76

Offside with #55

Modern Love

Charmed by the Bartender

Hooked by the Boxer

Mad about the Banker

Single Dads Club

Real Deal

Dirty Talker

Sexy Beast

Hollywood Hearts

Mister Mom

Animal Attraction

Domestic Bliss

Bedroom Games

Cold as Ice

On Thin Ice

Break the Ice

Chicago Law

Smitten with the Best Man

Tempted by my Ex-Husband

Seduced by my Ex's Divorce Attorney

Blue Collar Brothers

Flirting with Fire

Crushing on the Cop

Engaged to the EMT

White Collar Brothers

Sexy Filthy Boss

Dirty Flirty Enemy

Wild Steamy Hook-up

The Rooftop Crew

My Bestie's Ex

A Royal Mistake

The Rival Roomies

Our Star-Crossed Kiss

The Do-Over

A Co-Workers Crush

Plain Daisy Ranch

One Last Summer

The One I Left Behind

The One I Stood Beside

The One I Didn't See Coming

The Greene Family

My Twist of Fortune

My Beautiful Neighbor

My Almost Ex

My Vegas Groom

A Greene Family Summer Bash (Novella)

My Sister's Flirty Friend

My Unexpected Surprise

My Famous Frenemy

A Greene Family Vacation (Novella)

My Scorned Best Friend

My Fake Fiancé

My Brother's Forbidden Friend

A Greene Family Christmas (Novella)

Lake Starlight

The Problem with Second Chances

The Issue with Bad Boy Roommates

The Trouble with Runaway Brides

The Drawback of Single Dads